TEXARKANA PUBLIC LIBRARY

P9-DFD-034

ANGEL WITHOUT MERCY

By Anthea Cohen

ANGEL WITHOUT MERCY
ANGEL OF VENGEANCE
ANGEL OF DEATH

ANGEL
WITHOUT MERCY

ANTHEA COHEN

PUBLISHED FOR THE CRIME CLUB BY
DOUBLEDAY & COMPANY, INC.
GARDEN CITY, NEW YORK
1984

All of the characters in this book
are fictitious, and any resemblance
to actual persons, living or dead,
is purely coincidental.

Library of Congress Cataloging in Publication Data
Cohen, Anthea.
    Angel without mercy.
    I. Title.
PR6053.O34A8   1984   823'.914
ISBN 0-385-19104-9

Library of Congress Catalog Card Number 83–14060
Copyright © 1982 by Anthea Cohen
All Rights Reserved
Printed in the United States of America
First Edition in the United States of America

To Patricia Highsmith,
in admiration

2-13-84

87711

ANGEL WITHOUT MERCY

Nurse Carmichael peered from under the green shaded lamp that stood on her desk in the middle of the ward at the twelve cots surrounding her, evenly spaced along the walls.

Staff Nurse Carmichael hated the children's ward and hated the children. They were not communicators, she couldn't get through to them; they couldn't tell you if they'd got a stomach ache, or a headache, or a pain in the leg. Most of them just whimpered or wailed or yelled or stamped and went red in the face. She detested them, but of course she couldn't say so. A nurse who wishes for promotion does not detest children.

She looked round in case one of them should wake up and she would have to do something for it. The cots looked like little cages in the eerie blue of the electric night-light. There was, at the moment, nothing to worry about.

She listened to the heavy, rapid breathing of the little asthmatic in the bed near the door and behind her a child sobbed in its sleep, then settled again. She cocked her head to hear if there was any noise from the nursery where the smaller babies were, just outside and to the left of the ward door. Then, because she was so anxious, was always so anxious, she got up, walked to the nursery, and looked at each tiny body; six of them in smaller cots than those in the ward.

She walked round, keeping her torch light down so as not to disturb them. They were all sleeping. She dreaded that familiar noise that came from a baby before it actually started crying, the sniffs, and then the whimpering, and then the full open-mouthed blast of its small lungs; but there was nothing, all was quiet. She went back, partially satisfied, and sat down at her desk again looking at her watch as she did so.

Half-past three. Well, the night was going by. Eight o'clock —breakfast—a sharp walk—that was her habit. Then some reading, write a couple of letters, and bed. Nurse Carmichael relaxed a little, and some of her anxieties momentarily receded. She went on with her conscientious studying of the surgical book in front of her.

Old Mr. Machin, in Stenton ward, coughed harshly and noisily. Staff Nurse Hiram Jones making tea in the kitchen cursed him softly. He'd wake up the other old men, then they'd all start. When one coughed, they all coughed. The geriatric staff nurse didn't want his tea-making interrupted. He listened. Sure enough a cacophony of coughs started up, and just as he knew it would, a buzzer sounded.

Hiram went into the ward and saw the little red light above the bed indicating who had pressed the buzzer. It was old Mr. Machin who had started the coughing. He went up to him and said shortly, "Yes, what do you want?"

"Can I have a bottle, please?" the old man asked.

The staff nurse nodded and padded softly towards the sluice. As he walked away he wondered what had happened. After Miss Hughes had done her round he'd put a bottle by everybody's bed. She forbade that practice, but screw her. He thought he'd put one by Machin's bed.

He picked up a bottle from the rack in the sluice, gazed out of the window for a moment into the starlit night, then walked quietly back to the bed and handed the old man the urinal. "Here you are. Didn't I give you one after she'd been round? I thought I did," he said.

"Yes, you did—I spilt it in the bed." The old man's face was half accusatory, half apologetic.

"God in Heaven," said Hiram Jones and threw the bed-clothes back. "Better get out of bed." He helped the old man by pulling his legs over the side. Mr. Machin stood by the bed, bent double, not attempting to stand upright.

"There you are," he said and took a dressing-gown from behind the locker, slipped it over the bent shoulders, and Mr. Machin sat down heavily on the locker. Hiram padded off again and came back with clean sheets, a bucket, and a cloth. He stripped the sheets off, wiped the rubber pad dry, and remade the bed with the clean linen.

Hiram Jones put a clean night-shirt over the old man's outstretched arms and put him back to bed. "Well, don't do it again," he said. There was a little more sharpness to his voice now, not because he was bad-tempered but because he was tired, tired of his work on the geriatric ward. Tired of dirty beds which were more plentiful than clean ones; tired of the constant demands of the old people; tired of the way things were at home, as well as the way things were here, and just . . . tired.

Marion Hughes sat in her office. She didn't look tired. She looked as fresh, as efficient, as capable and trim as when she

had walked into the office at eight o'clock the night before
and had taken the report.

Miss Hughes, in common with nearly everyone else on
night duty at St. Jude's, frequently looked at her watch. She
did so now. It was four o'clock, tea-time. She put out her hand
and touched a bell beside her desk. Almost immediately the
door opened and a nurse popped her head round. "Yes, Miss
Hughes?"

"Your cap's on crooked, nurse." Marion Hughes hardly
looked up. It was difficult to know how she knew the nurse's
cap wasn't on straight; perhaps the nurse always wore her cap
like that. She put her hand up and straightened it. "Yes, Miss
Hughes," she said again.

"Would you ask Mrs. Upton to bring me up my tea and
biscuits, but not those terrible custard cream things. If she
brings those, she'll have to take them back. Tell her."

"Yes, Miss Hughes."

The nurse's head disappeared, and the door closed softly
behind her. It was as well to close Miss Hughes's door softly.
She didn't like noise.

Marion Hughes got up, walked across to the small wash-
hand basin she had particularly asked to be put into the night
duty room. She studied her face in the mirror above it. Her
dark hair was neat. She put up her hand and touched the bun
at the nape of her neck, then she peered forward, looking
more closely at her face to see if her mascara was smudged; it
wasn't. Not quite satisfied with her mouth, she reached for
her handbag from the table beside her, took out a lipstick, and
applied a tiny bit more to her lower lip. Then she pursed her
lips together to spread the lipstick evenly, put it back in her
handbag, and snapped the clasp decisively. She looked again
at her face with fascination; it was undoubtedly a beautiful
face, perfect in shape, her brow high, cool, and unfurrowed.
Her light blue eyes stared back at her as coldly as they looked

at everything else, without warmth. She herself acknowledged that as she looked, and as she did so, the eyes staring back at her became worried, and a slight crease appeared between her eyebrows. She put up a finger and hastily tried to smooth it out, but at the back of her mind she knew why her eyes had become worried, and her brow for a minute furrowed.

Marion Hughes despised women who said, "Oh it's not for want of chances that I haven't married. It's just that Mr. Right hasn't come along." In her own case she knew she could not have said that, even if she had wanted to. The chances had not come along—Mr. Right had appeared once or twice on her horizon, and she had begun to hope, and then just as rapidly he had disappeared. Why?

Marion Hughes was puzzled by her own inability to be coquettish.

She envied the young nurses when she saw them, or rather caught them, flirting with the porter or a new, handsome young house surgeon. She envied them their ease, their naturalness, their obvious ability to handle their femininity and sensuality without even thinking about it, while she, Marion Hughes, spinster, aged thirty-seven, in the company of men felt self-conscious, almost clumsy.

She turned away, having washed her hands and applied some hand lotion, hardly necessary. She had touched nothing but pen and paper the whole night. Her job was to supervise, not to nurse.

It isn't as if I hadn't tried, she thought with resentment. I joined that golf club, played quite a good game, but all the men who had been there were either young Adonises who wouldn't look at her because of her age, or randy old men. The bridge club had been a bore more than anything else. Although she was an efficient bridge player, all the men had been accompanied by determined wives, ready to fend anything off. That had been useless, too. She shook her head as if to rid herself of the memory and managed to switch her thoughts back to the hospital and night duty. Well, she could be pretty sure of promotion; she supposed that would have to satisfy her. Then quite suddenly Sir James Hatfield with his handsome profile flashed across her mind, his wife only five weeks dead, but after all, he was not young, he was eligible, he was . . . She dismissed that thought from her mind too and determinedly sat down at her desk and looked at the report she had written so far.

Her two rounds of the hospital earlier on had been uneventful. She had met and spoken with her junior supervisor, who sat in the room downstairs away from Miss Hughes; she too had had little to report. Not much in Casualty; no surgical or medical admissions; slightly unusual, but nice not to have had a tiring night. A knock came at the door.

"Come," Marion Hughes said crisply.

The door opened and a fat, elderly woman came in carrying a tray on which were a teapot, milk jug, and sugar-bowl, a plate with biscuits, a teacup with a brightly polished spoon resting in the saucer, all matching crockery, white with blue roses: Miss Hughes's own, personal property, kept in the kitchen specially for her. She would use no other; if any of it ever got broken Mrs. Upton felt that she would resign, leave, certainly not stay the rest of the night. She put the tray down on the night superintendent's desk, in the space that had been cleared for her, looking carefully for faults in the laying-out of the tray.

"Thank you Mrs. Upton. How is your leg?"

Marion Hughes always asked after your leg, or your back, or your headache, but Mrs. Upton felt that Miss Hughes didn't give a damn about your leg, or your back, or your headache; a few weeks ago when her leg was bad Miss Hughes hadn't hesitated about sending her back to the kitchen, down three flights of stairs, and back again, twice, because a small thing was wrong with her tray. The milk, she had said, looked slightly curdled, and the second time, she didn't like that particular kind of biscuit.

No, Miss Hughes wouldn't care, thought Mrs. Upton, she wouldn't care if you were suffering from a brain tumour, and she a nurse! Well—it takes all sorts, but she didn't like Miss Hughes. "Good night, then, or should I say Good morning?" she said, venturing a smile which was not returned. Marion Hughes merely nodded, started to pour out the tea, and Mrs. Upton, as usual, beat a hasty retreat. The farther she was away from Miss Hughes, the more comfortable she felt.

Hiram Jones walked round the male geriatric ward looking at everything carefully. It was 7:30 A.M. At seven thirty Miss Hughes did her round. She walked by the beds, criticizing, scrutinizing, but being charming to the patients.

Long-term patients labelled her a bitch. Those who had just arrived, or who had been there only a short time, thought her an angel, a wonderful lady. It was Hiram who bore the brunt of her caustic asides as she made her way round the ward.

This morning she arrived at seven thirty-two. "Good morning, Mr. Machin. How are you this morning, better I hope?" Her bright voice wafted over the old man, who hardly responded. He was one of those who disliked her; he knew her sort, he said. Miss Hughes and Hiram walked on a little. "Surely you could do something about that old man's appearance," she said.

The only answer Hiram could think of, the only answer she would take, was "Yes, Miss Hughes."

"See to it then."

A little farther on, the stock phrase again. "Good morning,

Mr. Kemp. I do hope you've had a good night and are feeling better." Then, the bed well passed, "Mr. Kemp looks positively filthy. Staff Nurse Jones, can't you make sure that he looks a little less disreputable in the morning; his pillowslip has got a great tear across it. Please try and see that the nurses don't put on torn linen. You know it should be folded and sent to the mending room."

Passing another old man, his hands suspiciously under the bedclothes, looking lecherously at her, she gave a short, sharp exclamation of disgust. "I should have thought you could have prevented that kind of thing, Nurse Jones."

There was always at the end of each sentence a little upward inflection that made it sound as if she were asking a question rather than making a statement. She was the only person in the hospital Hiram Jones knew who had that inflection, and he hated it.

On the children's ward, too, Nurse Carmichael was busy. She had told her junior nurse four times in the last hour to see if the six babies in the nursery were dry. This routine had at last stung the girl into saying, "It's no use, Staff, I know Miss Hughes is coming, and I know she puts her hand down the kids' beds to see if they're wet. If one of them pees at the last minute as she's going out of the ward, she'll know and come back and find it. Why bother? If they're wet, they're wet."

"You wait till you're in charge of a ward, that's all, nurse," Staff Carmichael snapped back at her, and dashed into the nursery and felt down the babies' cots herself, and said triumphantly, "That baby at the end, what's its name, baby Peters, he's wet. Change him, go on." She looked at her watch. "Change him. She'll be here in a minute."

"Glory be to God," said the nurse resignedly, going into the nursery and muttering to herself, "Who gives a sod whether she finds the baby is wet or not."

Nurse Carmichael heard her and called after her, "It'll go on your report, you know, if she finds things like that." At that moment Miss Hughes appeared at the ward door.

Marion Hughes always waited in the doorway of the ward till the nurse in charge came to her. She would never under any circumstances go and find the nurse, no matter how busy the ward, how busy the nurse. That was her policy.

"Good morning, Nurse Carmichael." She looked with contempt at the anxious face confronting her with its sharp, twitching nose, sandy-coloured eyelashes, and weak grey eyes behind round spectacles, the mouth which drooped a little at the corners.

Nurse Carmichael made a desperate effort to smile. "Good morning, Miss Hughes. I hope you've had a pleasant night."

Marion Hughes looked again at the woman in front of her and thought, with satisfaction, of her own image in the mirror upstairs.

She began her round of the children's ward, stopping at each cot. Some of the children bounced up and down and beamed at her, glad it was morning, glad the night was over, dark was gone. One or two of the sicker children gazed at her. They did not react. Marion Hughes looked at them, clicked her tongue a little, and her eyes remained exactly the same, without warmth.

"Charming," she said of a little girl, sitting up in her cot, thumb in mouth, golden curls falling down to her shoulders, brown eyes looking directly into the steely blue ones, perhaps for reassurance, but reassurance was not part of the commerce of Miss Hughes. She murmured again, "Charming little child," and walked on. Does she like children, Nurse Carmichael wondered, or does she dislike them as much as I do?

The familiar worry clouded Nurse Carmichael's thoughts again.

As if reading them, Marion Hughes turned to her. "You don't like the children's ward, do you, nurse? It's a pity, because after all it's part of the all-round nursing scene."

Nurse Carmichael stuttered, "Indeed I do, Miss Hughes, I love the little ch—children, I love the children's ward, nothing makes me happier than being on the children's ward, I love the little ones."

Miss Hughes turned round and faced Nurse Carmichael. "There's no need to say these things to me, Staff Nurse, I've known from the first night you were on here that you were quite incapable of communicating with children and did not particularly like them. However, you've only another week or so to do on the ward. It shouldn't worry you too much."

"Yes, Miss Hughes, just another couple of weeks."

Nurse Carmichael was routed. She had always thought she had put on a good show every time Marion Hughes came into the ward and that she had deceived her into thinking that this was a happy part of her nursing career, but she hadn't deceived her, not for a moment.

The deceit had been a desperate attempt, for she wanted so much to get a promotion. She was the other side of thirty. It was time, time for a sister's post. Others, younger, had been promoted ahead of her. She'd got to . . .

The sister of the women's surgical ward was leaving to get married, and Carmichael was going to apply for that post.

Nurse Carmichael to Sister Carmichael, to get away from the children, to get away from night duty, most of all to get away from Marion Hughes. In the woman's face she saw a whole dream disintegrating in front of her. A lot depended on the night superintendent's report, on all reports of course, but this one she had hoped would be good. She knew, as she looked into Miss Hughes's face, that it wouldn't be.

Carmichael was filled with contempt for herself, for the look of fondness she had put on every time Marion Hughes had come to the ward. She'd even manoeuvred some mornings to be standing with a baby in her arms, crooning to it. What was the use? She turned her face away. If her dislike of children was so apparent, her dislike of Marion Hughes must be also. It was better if she kept her eyes averted.

Hiram Jones slammed into his coat and said cheerio to the day staff nurse, who was taking over from him, and to whom he'd just given the night report.

"Don't take so much notice of her, Jones," said the day staff nurse.

"It's all very well for you, George. You don't have her all night hovering there, like some bloody big bird of doom."

"Oh, I've had my brushes with old Hughes, when she's carried on about work we'd left for the night staff, which she didn't think should have been left. I know her."

"It's not the same," said Hiram. "You don't have to take her round three times during the night, carping all the time, four times, if she's in the mood. One of these days I'll . . . one of these days . . ."

"One of these days, what? Stop thinking about her, you're off now, till tonight. Go out this morning on a drunk, that's the best thing to do, then have a good sleep."

"That's probably what I'll do. I'm so tired, I'll go out and get drunk. That'll probably make me feel better. That's what she does to you, drives you to drink. I tell you, one of these days . . ." He left the sentence unfinished and walked out of the ward, still muttering to himself. George, the day staff

nurse, followed him with sympathetic eyes for a second or two
and then turned back to the busy ward.

Carmichael went into the changing room and got out of her
uniform and into her tan frock and put over the top a camel-
hair coat. She could feel the tears pricking behind her eyelids
but wouldn't let them fall.

I won't let her make me cry—after all, she's not the only
one to report me. The other sisters have all found me . . .
She tried to stop thinking even about the other sisters; she
didn't want to think about it at all. She twitched the tail of
light brown hair over the back of her coat collar and stood
mechanically doing the buttons up. Then she began to think
of the seven-thirty round.

Two babies wet, one child with half its bowl of cornflakes
and milk in the bed. She'd begged the junior nurse to look
after that kid; she always threw her food about, beastly little
girl, the angelic-looking one too. Then the final, more serious
disaster. Miss Hughes had put her hand on the forehead of a
child lying rather listlessly in its cot. "This child feels as
though it has a temperature," she had said, looking directly at
Nurse Carmichael, then down at the chart, which stated that
an hour ago the child's temperature had been normal.

"Take it again, please," Miss Hughes had said, and Nurse
Carmichael had done so. The temperature had been 101.4.
What the hell had put that temperature up in an hour? Nurse
Carmichael knew she had taken it very carefully under the
blasted kid's arm. Perhaps she hadn't held it there long
enough. Anyway the temperature had been altered in the re-
port from normal to 101.4 in Miss Hughes's flourishing hand.
Everyone would know. The ward sister to whom she'd given

the report raised her eyebrows when she had come to this entry and looked up at Nurse Carmichael.

"How did that happen, Staff?"

Carmichael had only been able to shake her head miserably and say, "I don't know."

It didn't augur well for tonight, and it didn't augur well for promotion either. She slammed the changing-room door behind her, went along the corridor, down the stairs, and through the front hall, where the receptionist had just come in early to water her innumerable plants.

"Good night, Carmichael," the receptionist called out cheerfully. Carmichael barely nodded in reply, opened the inner door, went through the lobby, to the left of which was the switchboard operator's office. She glanced through and saw the operator sitting there with her nose in a magazine, the telephone ringing stridently beside her. She was obviously going to make the caller wait; let them think she was busy and couldn't answer the phone the moment it rang.

"That's a hospital," muttered Carmichael to herself nastily and walked out of the front door, closing it noisily behind her; then she strode across the hospital forecourt and out of the gate, towards the bus stop.

The little country town of Menton-on-Wye, which St. Jude's served with its 115 beds, was basking in the early morning sunlight.

The 115 beds were not often all in use, because the hospital was old, Victorian, and in need of repair. A roof leaked here, or something went wrong with the operating-theatre plumbing. A hazardous existence; but it was a hard-working hospital, with acute and geriatric beds, a conglomeration of medicine and surgery, and a conglomeration of surgeons and doctors to match.

The lawns round the hospital were fairly well tended, the beds planted with wallflowers, still straggly and thin in the cool morning; on the whole the scene was pleasing. The bronze bust of Queen Victoria over the front door, once bright, now green with age, looked benignly down on those leaving and entering.

On the right of the hospital the children's ward bulged out into a glass balcony, and the children were already running about laughing and screaming, glad to be free of the cage-like cots. Some of the ward windows were open now, and as the sun struck them, it showed that the outsides badly needed cleaning.

Soon the forecourt would be full of consultants' and visiting doctors' cars; at the moment it was empty.

Suddenly a big van, bearing the sterile supplies, lumbered through the IN entrance of the forecourt; at the same moment a red sports car careered through the OUT exit of the forecourt and drew up with a screech of tyres, its bonnet stopping an inch away from the hospital wall, as Nigel Denton, newly appointed registrar to St. Jude's, jammed on his brakes. He had been called in for an emergency, an appendectomy. This morning, apart from a round done yesterday, and a visit when he applied for the post, was all he knew of St. Jude's. Having arrived in dramatic fashion, he leaned back in the car and surveyed the scene, all the urgency of his entrance belied by his relaxed attitude.

Marion Hughes heard the screech of tyres on the forecourt asphalt and noted the red car coming through the wrong opening. The haste, the disorderly manner of the doctor's arrival, the fact that he now sat there after his display of urgency, all this offended her. She looked at him with distaste, closed the front door of the hospital behind her, and made her way down the steps.

"Good morning," she said coldly. "I presume you are Mr. Denton, the new surgical registrar?"

"How did you guess I was a surgeon? Why shouldn't I be a physician called to a cardiac arrest?" Denton infused a humorous note into the question.

Those cold, blue eyes appraised him. "I don't think you have the look of a physician, more that of a surgeon," said the night superintendent, her eyes fixed on his face.

"Haven't I seen you before, somewhere?" she went on.

"Surely that's my line," said Denton, again trying to make the scene lighter.

"May I suggest you hurry—the theatre staff are waiting for you." Marion Hughes's voice was cold. Her eyes lingered on his face a moment longer.

"Yes, I have seen you before somewhere," she said. "No doubt I shall remember." And she walked away.

Nigel levered himself up and swung his legs over the door of his car, stood upright, sprinted up the steps, and burst into the hospital front door. He poked his head through the small hatch of the door that led into the switchboard operator's office. She was filing her nails. The phone was ringing.

"Making them wait a bit?" said Nigel. "Making them think we're a great deal busier than we actually are? That's how it should be."

The operator looked up from her nails. "Yes," she said laconically.

"Who's that good-looking dame I met, coming out of the hospital just now? She spoke to me." Nigel Denton screwed up his face comically. "Yes, you could say she spoke to me. Just."

"Yes, it's like sucking lemons, isn't it, talking to our Miss Hughes," the switchboard operator said, a certain amount of sympathy in her voice, and then she added, "Who are you anyway?"

"Denton, new registrar," he answered. "Appointed three months ago. First day here yesterday. Didn't see much of it, though, haven't seen anybody much yet. Haven't seen you before. What's it like here anyway?"

"Unspeakable," said the operator, and went back to filing her nails.

The telephone had stopped ringing. Someone must have given up in despair.

"Ta for those encouraging words, angel," said Nigel and withdrew his head from the hatch, continued through into Reception, and then bounded up the stairs to the theatres.

The operating-theatres at St. Jude's were three flights up, situated at the top of the hospital. As Nigel reached their closed outer doors, he was slightly breathless.

Out of condition, old boy, he thought to himself. He glanced up, the words OPERATION IN PROGRESS were lit up. Hope it's not, he thought, and somebody got here before me.

He pushed open the main doors and found himself in a small lobby; on the left side a door leading to the recovery room, on the other the surgeons' changing room. Both doors were shut. He gently pushed open the theatre door in front of him, caught a glimpse of green-clad figures walking about and the black cushions of the theatre table on which shone down the round circle of the theatre light, when a voice said, "Shut that door, for God's sake. What do you think this is?"

He shut it, tentatively opened the door into the changing room, and looked round. There seemed no theatre gear put out for him, and the row of lockers offered no solution. He went out again into the lobby and pushed open the theatre doors more determinedly, and before anyone could speak said, "I'm the new surgical registrar, Denton. Where the hell are my theatre clothes?" He let the door swing to.

This brought some response. He had hardly strode back into the changing room when a nurse appeared at the door, clad in a short, green theatre dress and the paper hat with an elastic band, which successfully hid every scrap of hair. Her face was pale and spotty, and she looked very, very young.

"Mr. Denton?" she said. "Your locker's over there, the one without the label on. You should put on your own label. The boots are under the sink. Sometimes they're mixed up, see you don't get a six and a ten." She giggled, then put her hand up to her mouth as if she shouldn't have and murmured, "Sorry," and disappeared.

Just as Nigel was opening the door of his locker, she reappeared. "Don't hurry. Your case isn't even up yet," she said.

"But it's scheduled for eight thirty, and it's quarter to nine."

"I know, but Max is on. You see, if a case comes in before the night porter's off, he has to bring it up; that's the rule. Well, they made 'em. Anyway, he hasn't brought it up yet. See you later."

She remained standing, looking at him, chewing slightly; maybe, Nigel reflected, on a piece of breakfast toast that had got lodged behind a tooth and had just emerged.

"Want to see me undress?" he said when she didn't move. "Or am I allowed a tiny bit of privacy as a new surgeon who's just arrived and is about to perform the first operation he has ever done in his life?"

"That's not true," said the nurse, still chewing.

"No," he amended. "That is not strictly true. I have done a couple and seen a lot on the telly. So, with your assistance, this patient should emerge from the operation, we hope successfully. Now, get." She got.

Nigel Denton walked into the scrubbing-up area of the operating-theatre, which was divided from the main part by a large sheet of glass, through which he could see the still empty theatre table, the circle of light shining in the middle. At the scrubbing-up sink next to his was a girl or woman. It was difficult to tell in her theatre gear, mask and cap, whether she was young or old, but he thought he saw a trace of grey hair peeping out from under the side of the cap.

"I'm June Fyldes, theatre superintendent. I thought I'd scrub for you, seeing it's your first day here." Her eyes smiled at him over her mask. She was the most pleasant person he'd met at St. Jude's up to now.

"Thanks. You only scrub for the mighty consultants, eh?"

"I wouldn't say that," said June Fyldes, scrubbing busily at her arms up to the elbows. "But now and again I feel it's my duty to look after the newcomer." By her eyes he could tell she was smiling again.

"Thanks," he said. At that moment, through the glass, he saw the theatre doors open and a trolley being wheeled in, propelled at one end by a grey-coated porter he judged to be Max of nightduty fame, at the other end by the grace of God. As the trolley came to rest accurately beside the theatre table, one of the green-clad theatre nurses took hold of the poles and lifted with the porter; the patient was transferred easily enough from trolley to table. Nigel went on scrubbing.

He watched the porter draw the poles out from the canvas stretcher on the theatre table and place them with a slight clanking noise, wood on wood, on the trolley; then he took off the blankets covering the patient and put these on the trolley too. A theatre nurse came forward with a light blanket and covered the patient.

The porter was about to back out of the door when a nurse called out, "Don't forget the pillow. You'll have Sister Dench after you." The porter came back and took the pillow from under the patient's head. A nurse replaced it with a theatre pillow, and out the trolley went.

"Who's giving the anaesthetic?" Nigel asked June Fyldes.

"Oh, that will be Dr. Mayhew," she said. "He's nearly always called early in the morning, but he doesn't mind; he's a local G.P. A good anaesthetist. Ah, there he is," she said, as a man walked through the theatre doors. She nodded to him. Dr. Mayhew raised an arm in salute through the glass to her and then went towards the patient.

They finished scrubbing up. By the time they went through into the theatre the patient was anaesthetized, and Dr. Mayhew was just removing a needle from the vein and bending the arm up with a swab firmly placed in the crook of the elbow.

The nurses positioned the patient, removed the blanket, and green towels were spread all over the body. It became anonymous except for the small part of the abdomen which was to be opened.

Dr. Mayhew pulled the anaesthetic machine closer to the head of the operating table, put a mask over the patient's nose and mouth, and strapped it expertly in place. He looked up at Nigel and June Fyldes, nodded, then ensconced himself on a stool at the end of the table by the patient's head, spread a book on his lap, and started reading, while the bag on the machine beside him puffed gently in and out. All looked efficient and organized. Nigel Denton stood poised with a knife in his hand, and June Fyldes stood on a box on the other side of the patient, as she was shorter than Denton. Both looked at the anaesthetist again.

"O.K. to start?" asked Denton, and Dr. Mayhew looked up, glanced at the patient, nodded, and Nigel Denton stroked his knife gently down the known area in which the offending appendix lay, and a small, thin line began to bleed gently. The operation had started and Denton felt suddenly at home.

Everything went smoothly. Nigel Denton thought the theatre staff seemed efficient. Of course it was daytime, with full staff. He wondered what operating at night would be like. He looked up at June Fyldes and then down again at the incision.

"What's it like at night?" he asked. "If you have to operate, I mean."

"O.K.," she said, busy swabbing for him, the sucker going noisily, drawing the blood away from his retractors and away from the open wound. "It's O.K."

Dr. Mayhew looked up and chimed in, "As long as you keep out of the way of Marion Hughes."

"Marion Hughes, who's that?" said Denton. "Oh, I believe I met her this morning."

"The biggest bitch walking."

Denton looked up at the anaesthetist in surprise; there was so much dislike in the remark. Somehow one didn't expect it from Dr. Mayhew's benign expression; but a quiet remark from June Fyldes, "Now Dr. Mayhew, let him form his own opinion," made him close the subject and say no more.

He finished the operation, put the sutures in deftly, and June Fyldes dabbed the wound quickly, to dry it off. The bleeding had stopped. A piece of strapping was put over it, the nurses began to take off the towels, and Denton walked out of the theatre. He'd love a brandy, he thought, almost smiling at himself. Of course, it was a ludicrous thought, he'd given all that up, but God, how he would love a brandy.

You've only taken out an appendix, for God's sake, he muttered to himself, alone in the changing room, and you want a brandy. It's ten o'clock in the morning. Have a brandy now, and get that smell on your breath when the chief comes in. That will be a good start.

"Coffee, doctor?" A nurse put her head round the door.

He nodded. "Please," he said.

A little later she came in with a cup of coffee, which had slopped into the saucer, and plonked it down on the table. "Courtesy of the theatre," she said and walked out.

Nigel sat down on the side of the table, straightening his tie as he did so, and then picked up the cup and sipped the coffee. It was lukewarm and tasted of metal. He drank it because there was nothing else.

June Fyldes poked her head round the door. "Know where the canteen and everything is?" she asked.

He nodded.

"O.K.," she said. "You'll be meeting Sir James Hatfield this morning."

"The great Sir James," said Nigel. "I haven't met him yet. He was away at my interview, and away yesterday. Holiday?"

"No, he lost his wife. She died about a month, five weeks ago," said June Fyldes. "He had a month off."

"Nice man to work for?" asked Nigel, draining the rest of the terrible coffee.

"No," said June Fyldes and left it at that.

"Good surgeon, then?" asked Denton.

June Fyldes looked at him levelly and said, "Not particularly. I don't think I'd better say anything else. The others are O.K.," she added as a rider. "Sir James, of course, is senior surgeon. His title makes things dodgy." She nodded to him in a friendly fashion and went back into her domain, leaving Nigel to go down and find his way round the wards, introduce himself to the sisters, and try to get some knowledge of the surgical patients before Sir James or the other general surgeon appeared.

Some task, and not even a brandy, he thought. He already felt weary, as if he'd done a full day's work. Maybe it was the newness of the place, and he'd soon feel better. He hoped so.

When Hiram Jones arrived home, John wasn't there. Hiram always hated this. The little flat seemed empty and lonely when John wasn't there to say, "Had a good night?"

Hiram went through into the kitchen, opened the refrigerator, took out a bottle of milk, and swigged at it straight from the bottle. He turned round and caught a reflection of himself in the small mirror beside the kitchen door. He had a white moustache made by the milk. He wiped his mouth hastily. John didn't like him drinking out of milk bottles. He put the top back on and quickly returned the milk to the refrigerator and closed the door. At that moment John came through the front door, slamming it behind him. He looked into the kitchen and saw Hiram.

"Home, Hiram, home from the hills?" he said.

"Where have you been, John, this early in the morning?" asked Hiram.

John answered in a singsong voice that Hiram always found particularly irritating. "Out all night, my love; on the tiles with the boys and girls, dancing the night away." Then he came through and faced Hiram in the kitchen, his face belligerent. "And why the hell shouldn't I be?"

"I didn't say anything," answered Hiram mildly.

"No, but you bloody looked it," said John. His face became more petulant. His lower lip stuck out, like a spoiled child deprived of something. Hiram could never make up his mind whether he loved him more when he looked like that or less. Suddenly, for no reason at all that Hiram could think of, his thoughts switched to Marion Hughes. Did she know about him and John? Did she consider him as a poof and dismiss it at that? He expected so; then again John broke into his thoughts.

"Any of the little pilly willies then? Manage to get any last night?" He sidled up to Hiram.

"I had a hell of a night last night with that bloody woman. Four rounds she did on my ward, three on everybody else's, and she found fault every time she came."

"The darling Miss Hughes, rearing her ugly head again," said John, pirouetting his way across the kitchen. "That doesn't stop you getting a few pilly willies, darling, does it, for God's sake? I could do with something, I feel a bit high. I need to sleep today, as well as you."

Hiram put his hand into his trouser pocket and took out an envelope.

"There are a few in here," he said.

John opened it. "Oh, goody goody, not many, but some at least."

"I'm getting scared, scared that bitch will ask how many pills they had the night before. Somebody's going to tell. Someone will say they didn't have any," said Hiram.

"You can always say they're demented, out of their tiny minds, Hiram. Half of them are, you're so slow-witted," said John, and he put a couple of the capsules into his mouth.

"I'm going to beddy-byes, now. Night-night." He walked into his bedroom and slammed the door behind him.

Hiram sighed wearily, dropped onto the kitchen chair, and lit a cigarette. Again a nasty vision of those blue eyes of

Marion's floated into his mind and he thought, I wonder what she'd do, if she knew I was taking pills home for John instead of giving them to the patients. I wonder what she'd do. Suddenly he stubbed his cigarette out, half-finished, on the top of the Formica table, got up, and said aloud violently, "If only that bitch wasn't there. If only she wasn't there. If only I didn't have to face her every single damn night, except when it's her night off." He could almost hear her voice with those upward inflections, "Stealing drugs, Staff Nurse Jones?" He could almost hear it.

"I bring her home with me, I dream about her," he muttered. "I'll take two pills myself and go to bed, and I won't go out and get drunk. What's the good, she'll only come with me, I won't forget her."

Nurse Carmichael came out of the hospital gates, walked across the road, and waited in the chilly morning air for her bus. When it arrived, she got on, took the ten minutes' ride, eyes down looking neither to right nor left, not interested in anything but her own problems. She knew she had lost a lot of ground last night, a lot of ground. Miss Hughes would . . .

Carmichael tried to brush the woman out of her mind. For goodness' sake forget it, she thought, and got off the bus at her stop. She walked down the street to the house where she had her bed-sitting room. At the front door she got her key out of her handbag and was about to put it in the lock when the door opened and a man stood back to allow her to enter.

"Good morning, Mr. Stokes," Carmichael simpered.

He was a good-looking young man and answered without looking at her, with early morning gruffness. "Good morning, Miss—er—," and passed her without a glance.

She sighed. Ever since he'd moved in she'd liked the look of him. Perhaps he was a little younger than she, but—he might be lonely. She'd thought of going and knocking on his door and asking to borrow something, a jug of milk or—but she hadn't.

Two children rushed down the second flight of stairs and nearly knocked her over. She ascended the last flight and came to the door of her own room. It had been scratched again. The kids did it with coins, the little bastards. No wonder she hated them. A door opened a couple of doors along and a hand came out, grabbed a bottle of milk, and disappeared again, the door closing with a small, distinct bang. It was strange that whenever she heard a door open or shut she felt more lonely. She let herself into her own room, shut that door, and leaned up against it for a moment. She felt tired, not exactly physically tired, but mentally tired. She thought, I'm tired because of Miss Hughes, because I've lost the chance of promotion. I'm not a bad nurse, I'm a good nurse, but when she treats you like that it undermines you. That's what I am, undermined. Blast her.

She wondered what the other people on night duty at St. Jude's were doing, now that, like her, the morning had set them free. She often thought this as she wandered about her bed-sitting room, doing the small chores. How many of them were alone in bed-sitters? Some of them had husbands and children to go home to; others were shacked up, as they put it, with a boy-friend, with a young husband. She wondered if those who were alone, like her, hated it as much as she did.

A sister's post—more money—she could start a mortgage on a small bungalow with a garden—she could have a cat, she'd always wanted a cat; they didn't mind waiting for you to come home, they welcomed you, that's what she wanted, something, someone, to welcome her.

That bitch would queer it all, if she got the chance, queer it all with a bad report. If only she could stop her, but she couldn't stop Miss Hughes. It was like trying to stop the tide turning. She made come coffee, automatically took the textbook out of her bag, put it on the table, and sat down in front of it. She must go on learning, trying never to be caught out. She must, she must. The print swam in front of her eyes, but determinedly she looked up, blinking, took a long drink of coffee, and then stared down at the page again.

Marion Hughes parked her car outside the block of flats where she lived. Luckily they hadn't got round to meters yet. There was a space reserved in front of each building for people who lived inside, theoretically at least. Often it was full but this morning she was lucky.

She went briskly up the steps, in the front door and walked up the three flights to her flat. There was an OUT OF ORDER notice on the lift. Marion grimaced slightly to herself. Right, she thought, I'll mention that when I next pay my rent at the estate agents. I'm not paying for amenities that don't exist. She let herself into her flat, looked round with satisfaction at the immaculate, prettily decorated hallway.

She went into the sitting-room, crossed over immediately to the record-player, and put on some Mozart. It started up loudly, and because of her neighbour she turned it down to a more gentle tone. The she went through to the kitchen to make coffee.

As she waited for the kettle to boil, Nigel Denton's face flashed in front of her again. Sir James won't like him, she thought. He's not the kind of man I like, either; there's something about him that's vaguely familiar. Where have I seen him before? Certainly not when he came for the interview—

that would be during the day. She tried to shake the memory out of her mind. It would come back to her; it usually did. She was proud of her memory, her ability to docket information and keep it. The kind of mind she possessed had served her well in nursing.

The kettle clicked automatically; it had boiled. She took some instant coffee and powdered milk from the cupboard and made herself a cup of coffee, stirring it reflectively. The thoughts of this morning when she looked at herself in the mirror came back to her.

Eligible men, of the right age, there weren't all that many; certainly outside hospital she met very few. She thought again of the golf club crowd, of the bridge crowd. Most of the women in the bridge club were older that she, and their husbands were firmly attached. One or two of them had made a pass at her but that wasn't what she wanted. She wanted security, position, prestige, to be kept in a manner—she looked round her spacious sitting-room—better than she could keep herself, or else where was the point?

Sir James Hatfield . . . Yes. He was really the only eligible man she knew, the only one she could settle for. A title, money. One would be proud, she thought, to be seen walking into a restaurant with him. He would know how to treat the waiter, how to order wine. Yes, those things were important. Her mind wandered on pleasantly to the background music. Lady Hatfield. Yes, she'd settle for that. How to do it? How did you do it? Ring him up a little later and ask him to dinner perhaps, on the pretext that one thought he might be lonely, missing his wife—there'd be crowds of people to do that. But . . . no, he must see more of her, she must engineer it. Being on night duty was a disadvantage; she didn't see him often enough. She must make sure, somehow, that she did. She finished her coffee.

Nigel Denton walked into the junior doctors' Common Room and looked round. There were papers piled up on the window-sill, a mass of case notes on the table, and for some unknown reason, an empty egg box. A television in the corner, chairs drilled like soldiers round the wall; the carpet was a peculiar puce shade and the walls pink. The whole thing made him feel slightly bilious. He sank down in one of the chairs and found it surprisingly comfortable, then noticed by the walled-in fireplace, before which stood an electric fire with artificial log effect, a bell. He pushed it. Sometime later a face appeared round the door.

"Yes?"

"Is it possible for me to have a pot of coffee?" Nigel asked. "I've just been operating and . . ."

"Yes," said the face and disappeared.

He waited and before long the face came back, this time attached to a green overall, carrying a tray with two large pots on it, one of coffee and one of milk, both surprisingly hot, a bowl of sugar, and a cup and saucer. The woman plonked it down in front of him and disappeared without a word. Nigel poured out a cup of coffee and added milk.

Bugger Sir James, he thought and looked at his watch. Not a single consultant turned up yet, and it was half-past-bloody-eleven. What time do they turn up here? He took a flask from his pocket, poured some brandy into his coffee, and sipped it appreciatively. At that moment the door burst open and a young doctor came in, a stethoscope protruding from his pocket. He, too, pressed the bell and sniffed the air.

"Brandy in the coffee, new hospital rule is it?" he said, looking at Nigel, one eyebrow raised comically.

"I felt I needed it," said Nigel defensively. "Nigel Denton, new surgical registrar."

"Yes, I know. My name's Hayward, George Hayward. I'm the medical house officer. Hell of a job. Up, time and again in the night, like last night; had the Asian doctor on, made a balls of it, admitted a chap to Intensive Care, the one that you operated on this morning."

He imitated an Asian voice, "I thought it was coronary pain, doctor." Then he went on normally. "He's not a bad fella, but the trouble is I don't know what he learned over there in India about anatomy. He can't seem to differentiate between the right iliac fossa and the chest. Easily done though, I've done it myself. Silly bugger. Got me out of bed. I took one look, put my hand on the man's abdomen, and he nearly jumped out of bed. Got him removed to the surgical ward, and you came in."

"You won't know Dr. Percival Whitehouse, yet?" he went on. "Pray God, you won't. He's a fool, my chief. He thinks he knows it all. He'd still be using kaolin poultices if he had the chance. He's rising sixty-five, looks eighty. Don't know when he'll retire—I hope soon. They have to retire at sixty-five, you know, but they don't. They hang on, any old excuse will do. They totter around, for all I know some of them carrying leeches in a plastic bag in their pockets."

Nigel Denton laughed for the first time that day. He felt he'd found St. Jude's comic relief.

"Got any brandy left?" asked George. Nigel nodded and took out the flask from his pocket and splashed some into the house physician's coffee, which had just arrived.

"Now we'll stink of drink when the chiefs come in," said George cheerfully. "And they'll accuse us of being dipsomaniacs. The best reply you can make to that is what I always make to everybody. 'Yes, sir. You're right, sir.' "

Nigel laughed again. "Is there much night surgery?" he asked. "And do I have to do it all?"

"Most of it, mate," said George. "And working here in this sweet little hospital at night is hell, and I'll tell you why. It's because of one person, called the Night Super. She's not a nice lady, she's a bitch. She's somebody I would cheerfully murder, and I would have many accomplices."

"The one with the blue eyes?" said Denton.

"Met her already?" asked George, sipping his coffee with enjoyment.

"Hardly," said Nigel. "I just happened to pass her coming out of the hospital this morning. I'll no doubt meet her tonight if anything turns up. She didn't strike me as being overly pleasant."

"Overly pleasant!" George threw back his head and laughed. "You'll meet her tonight all right. You're expected to do a ten o'clock round. You'll meet her, and if she falls senseless at your feet with sensual pleasure, I shall be bloody surprised."

"Don't think I've got the looks for it, eh?" said Denton.

"Not that," said George. "Not that at all, mate. She's after bigger fish than you and me."

Four days went by, and Nigel got to know the various personalities in St. Jude's a little better. He met his two chiefs, Gordon Mayes and Sir James Hatfield. The former was a youngish consultant, obviously feeling his way in a newish job, still a little in awe of Sir James Hatfield. They could both take private patients. It was obvious that Sir James was the master in that particular field. Of the eighteen beds allotted to all surgeons, including the ear, nose, and throat man, the gynaecologist, and the orthopaedic surgeons, Sir James usually managed to fill at least eight beds and often managed to snatch a bed from the enraged E.N.T. surgeon. However, that kind of behaviour was not rare, and Nigel Denton had met it before at other hospitals.

On the third night, Nigel met the renowned and disliked Miss Hughes. He had heard her talked of by the nurses on day duty. He had even been warned by one attractive ward sister that he had better beware of her; he took little notice. He was used to night superintendents and their like, but when he came face to face with her at last, he realized she was not a run of the mill night super.

He had been lucky in getting no night calls for the first two nights and had escaped meeting her on his ten o'clock round, which was an obligatory part of St. Jude's routine as George Hayward had warned him. On the third night, however, that changed.

The night casualty officer, a rather mousy but pleasant woman, had asked him, when they were having coffee in the Common Room one evening, if it would be possible for him to relieve her one night on Casualty, as she wanted to go for an interview, and the hospital to which she was going was situated in a town too far distant for her to get back the same night.

"Don't you like St. Jude's, then?" Nigel asked.

"No, I've been here two years and that's enough. Too many unpleasant things have happened. I'm not going to get a casualty consultancy here, and that's what I want. The post I'm trying for isn't a consultancy, but it might lead to one. I don't see how I can get there and back in time to cover, unless you're kind enough to do it for me."

Nigel nodded. "Of course I will. It won't kill me to do twenty-four hours once in a while," he told her.

The casualty officer thanked him gratefully and pushed her hair wearily back from her forehead.

"It's been a rotten night," she told him. "And I had that bloody superintendent to battle with too. We had a car crash in; a bit of a pile up. There were four cars involved, not all that many people hurt, four or five, three seriously, the others minor injuries, but she must be there, just in case she feels there is anyone or anything she should know about."

"I haven't had the joy of meeting the lady yet; only just seen her passing as she went out of the hospital," Nigel said. "I can't say I'm looking forward to it."

"No, she's a bad influence in the place, a really bad influence. If you get someone like that at the top, someone absolutely unscrupulous, it filters right down through the night staff. She'll report anything to anybody."

"Strong language," said Nigel. "I've heard she's a bit of a tyrant. Is she that bad?" The casualty officer nodded.

"That bad. I feel she's so devious, she's like an eel with grease on it. I can't ever grasp what she's thinking or what she's going to do next. She reported me one night to Dr. Whitehouse. She said I'd let a patient go home who should have been admitted."

"A nurse, questioning a clinical decision? Come on," said Nigel.

The casualty officer nodded.

"Yes, I did let him go home. He had chest pains. I did an E.C.G. and couldn't find a single thing to point to it being coronary pain. In fact the man's father had died recently, and I felt that he was feeling the father's pain with a large functional overlay. Anyway, we were desperate on medical, extra beds up everywhere, and I let him go home."

"Did anything happen to him?"

"No, nothing. He was perfectly all right, but dear Miss Hughes reported it by letter to Dr. Whitehouse."

"So what?" Nigel argued. "You sent a letter to the man's G.P., didn't you? That would cover you."

"It does, and it doesn't," the casualty officer answered. "I had decided that the man's chest pains weren't of any significance; he might never go near his doctor. I told the patient to go and see him of course, but you know what they are. It's things like that though that have made me feel I want to get out of here and get another job. That and the fact that I'd like a consultancy in Casualty. Sometimes, though, I think it's purely because of Marion Hughes—feeble isn't it?"

Nigel privately thought it was feeble, but he didn't say so. He just said, "Not altogether, I've heard of a nurse behaving like that, reporting doctors. Just let her do something like that to me."

"She might, you certainly never know, she might. Anyway, the note she wrote to Dr. Whitehouse was so carefully worded. It got to me through George Hayward, who's a love, by the way. Have you met him?"

Nigel nodded. "I wouldn't put it quite like that, but he's a nice lad. What the hell did she put in the letter to your chief?"

"Something like—She felt slightly worried about the patient who had been in Casualty the night before with chest pains, and in her long experience she thought he should have been admitted for observation, as it was so easy for a tragic misdiagnosis to happen, and the onus of course would fall on the senior physician. Of course old Whitehouse, being the senior physician, is not the firmest of men and he fell for it. He sent for the man to come up to the clinic. Oh, everything was O.K. I was right, she was wrong, but somehow she makes it appear that she's right and caring and you're wrong and not caring. I expect you think we're catty women, rowing. But you'll see."

Nigel was to see, on that third night when he was covering for her in Casualty.

It was a pretty quiet night, Nigel had done his ten o'clock round and then decided to wait in the Common Room for calls. He had told Casualty where he was. Nothing happened for some time and he was dozing comfortably in the chair when at last the phone rang.

"There's a road accident in, doctor." The nurse didn't sound particularly harassed or worried.

"What is it?" he asked.

"Chap skidded, I think. The police are here with him. He's not drunk or anything by the look of it. He's got a compound fracture of his right leg."

"All right, I'll be down," said Nigel.

He came into Casualty to find the usual couple of ambulance men, chatting away in the waiting-room; he walked through and examined the patient. The man was young and fit but obviously in great pain. Nigel ordered a sedative and gently placed the green towel back over the mutilated leg. While the nurse was getting the sedative he looked at the man's written particulars—George Howell, age thirty-three, he read, and his address underneath. Nigel left the couch side and went out into the waiting-room to speak to the ambulance men. At that moment Miss Hughes walked through the plastic doors.

"Good evening, Mr. Denton," she said and nodded to the ambulance men.

"What have you brought us?" she asked.

"R.T.A., miss," said the senior ambulance man. "Not too bad, though; banged his car into a tree."

"Drinking?" said Marion Hughes.

"No, I don't think so." The ambulance man shook his head.

"How did he come to go into a tree? There's no ice out there, is there?"

"No, loose gravel, I think. It just slithered the car round into a tree. A lovely job too, that car; new Rolls, would you believe it? If it were mine I should be sitting on the dashboard weeping, never mind my leg."

"A Rolls?" Marion Hughes immediately became attentive. "I'll speak to him. I'll have a word with the patient," she said.

Nigel Denton grinned. This was a syndrome he was pretty used to: the night super or the Casualty day nurse watching out for patients for her favourite consultant. Well, the man in there hadn't particularly struck him as being a Rolls owner. He'd wait and see.

Marion Hughes went through into the Casualty area. Nigel followed her. She went up to the couch where the patient lay waiting for the porters to take him to X-ray, then to the ward. The nurse was in the process of giving him his anti-tetanus, and the sedative ordered by Nigel.

"Good evening, Mr. Howell." Marion Hughes's voice was charming. The nurse looked up, met Nigel's eye, and grimaced. She knew the score too.

Nigel saw on the next couch a man's coat and cap. He realized with delight that the patient was a chauffeur. He gently pulled the curtain along a little so that Miss Hughes should not see them and have cause to interrupt her charm act.

"I'm so sorry this happened. The ambulance man tells me you have such a lovely car, what a shame. And your leg . . ." She looked up at Nigel.

"Broken, I'm afraid. He'll have to be admitted. I have told him." There was a glint of laughter in his eyes, which he tried to hide. Marion Hughes noticed it and looked at him suspiciously, then the man answered her.

"My car?" he said. "It's the boss's. I was only driving it home for him."

"I see." Marion Hughes froze, then twitched back the curtain she had seen Nigel draw. He knew she realized he had done it to hide the chauffeur's cap and coat. She walked out of the cubicle and out of Casualty without another word.

One up to me, he thought, or should I say another pin going to be stuck into my wax image.

A few nights later Marion Hughes was in her office. She had reread the night report and was gazing in front of her, wondering just how long it would take for circumstances to arise in the order she wanted.

It was strange that no case had come in that demanded consultant surgery; a fractured leg had of course needed the orthopaedic surgeon, but she was not interested in him. It had to be Sir James Hatfield and no one else. She was determined, and yet nervous of her determination, frightened of a rebuff. As she thought about it she realized she had probably put her finger on the exact spot where her inadequacy with men lay. She was basically frightened of being rebuffed. She smiled to herself and wondered what a psychiatrist would make of that; an "overdominant mother," perhaps. Well, that was true enough, she had been overdominant, her mother, and getting away from home and into training had been a great relief.

As if in answer to her wish, the phone rang. "Miss Hughes?" It was the casualty staff nurse, an insipid girl, who was nervous of Miss Hughes and her criticism and tried hard to get everything right.

"There's a patient been admitted, Miss Hughes. The doctor, Miss Creasey, thinks she has a ruptured spleen. She's rather shocked, and is to be admitted straightaway to the women's surgical ward; she had a car accident."

"Well, nurse? Is this something you can't handle? Surely . . ." Marion Hughes's voice had its usual scornful overtones, the upward inflection very marked.

"Oh no, Miss Hughes," the unctuous voice went on. "I can handle it perfectly well. It's just that the lady's name is"—she paused, as if for effect—"Lady Marshall, and I thought, well —should she be sent to the women's surgical, do you think, or shouldn't the private floor be suggested? I didn't quite like to . . . What do you think, Miss Hughes? I thought it better to let you know."

"I'll come down to Casualty right away." Marion Hughes put the phone down firmly. This might be the opportunity for which she was waiting. She looked at her notice board to see who was consultant on call for such cases. It was Gordon Mayes. Well, she could get round that easily enough, as long as that fool Creasey hadn't phoned Nigel Denton yet but only the ward and the theatre. She felt sure that Nigel Denton could handle a ruptured spleen with ease, but he wasn't going to get the chance if she could stop it.

She walked into Casualty, the waiting-room plastic doors slapping behind her. There was a couple sitting there, the man nursing a finger with blood showing through the bandage. Miss Hughes pushed open the Casualty door, noting that the white paint was covered in black finger-marks and deciding that that would go in the report in the morning.

"Casualty is the front door of the hospital; really, I do think the sister should see it is kept clean." Something like that; it showed you had your eyes about you.

She closed the door of the waiting-room behind her. The

casualty staff nurse stood looking at her, her mouth drawn down in anxiety; then she spoke.

"I hope I did right, Miss Hughes. I didn't want to bring you down here for nothing, but I thought . . ."

"You did perfectly right," said Miss Hughes, glancing briefly at the nurse's face and giving her a tight smile. She had done the right thing and indeed might have to do it again before the circumstances were quite right for Miss Hughes, but she hoped this was the time. She would remember this nurse favourably when the report was to be made on her night duty behaviour.

"Leave it to me; I'll handle this. Has the doctor been informed? Not yet?"

"Um-m, not yet, Miss Hughes; Miss Creasey asked me to ring Mr. Denton . . ."

"But you haven't yet, nurse. Get Sir James Hatfield on the phone."

"Me, Miss Hughes?" The nurse sounded terrified. It was not usual for a nurse to ring a consultant; it was left to the casualty officer, but this time Miss Hughes was in charge.

She walked to where the patient was being examined in the main Casualty department. She saw a middle-aged woman, looking very white, lying on the couch anxiously watching the doctor's face. Miss Creasey was obviously trying to reassure her and turned in surprise as Marion Hughes approached. It wasn't time for her round, and the doctor wondered how she had known that the patient was in. Then it flashed across her mind. The nurse. She had asked her to phone Denton, but she'd phoned Miss Hughes. They must have some understanding between them.

"I was just explaining to Lady Marshall that we shall have to admit her," she said, watching Marion Hughes's face carefully.

A junior nurse at the other side of the couch moved to the

head and took the patient's hand, as the superintendent drew the casualty officer away.

"May I have a word with you?" said Marion Hughes softly. They walked through into the lobby.

"I think as this patient is titled we should suggest the private ward to her, and that means getting in a consultant, you realize."

"Oh yes, I hadn't thought of that. I was really more concerned about the patient's condition," said Miss Creasey.

"Of course. Don't worry. I told nurse to ring Sir James Hatfield."

"He's not on call. Mr. Mayes is," said Miss Creasey quickly.

"Oh, didn't you know? He's got a dinner engagement. Sir James is covering for him."

"No, I didn't know," said the casualty officer, her voice full of disbelief. She'd met this kind of thing before but not done so flagrantly. In one hospital in which she had worked she had found out that one of the nurses constantly called in the same G.P. to cover Casualty, whether he was on call or not, so that he got the resulting fee; but this, this was too much.

"Well," said Miss Hughes easily, "they can't inform everybody. Maybe they didn't consider it necessary to inform you."

Jane Creasey felt her face colouring. She was about to say more when the nurse returned from telephoning.

"Sir James says he'll be here directly, Miss Hughes," she said and glanced fearfully at the casualty officer.

"Isn't it customary, nurse, for the doctor to ring the consultant?" said Miss Creasey angrily. The nurse looked enquiringly at Miss Hughes as if for protection, and got it.

"I'm sure nurse was a little overanxious," said Miss Hughes. "You'd better go to the patient, nurse." The staff nurse hastily slipped past them both, sensing the turbulence in the air, went through into the Casualty area and back to Lady Marshall.

"Perhaps you would like to ring him now. I'm sure he'd appreciate it if he hasn't already left. I'm sorry nurse jumped the gun a little. She is rather an overanxious young woman, isn't she?" Miss Hughes's voice was challenging. The two women's eyes met.

"Unless perhaps you told her to ring him. Did you?" Miss Creasey's voice was trembling with rage.

"Are you insinuating that I'm trying to get private patients for Sir James Hatfield? This is a very serious insinuation indeed, Miss Creasey." Those steely blue eyes remained fixed on the casualty officer, and the beautiful mouth closed firmly like a trap and drew out into a straight line.

"No, I'm not insinuating anything. I'm merely saying that . . ."

The door of the waiting-room opened and a patient put his head round. "Will I have to wait much longer? I've been here half an hour, and my finger is still bleeding."

"Of course not. Yes, it's your finger, isn't it? Has nurse taken your particulars?" The man nodded. Miss Hughes went on placatingly.

"Come through and sit down by the doctor's desk. I'm sure she's ready for you now." She went to the phone and dialled.

"Private floor," she said. "We have a case coming up to you, Lady Marshall. She may be for immediate surgery. We've notified Sir James." She put the phone down and turned again to look at Dr. Creasey, but Dr. Creasey was no longer looking at her; it was useless, she knew that, and Marion Hughes knew that she knew it.

She turned again to the phone, to ring the theatre and alert Nigel Denton that he would be assisting Sir James.

"Let's have a look at this finger," Dr. Creasey said resignedly.

Marion Hughes's face relaxed. She went through the Casualty area and called, "Nurse, come and help doctor. Nurse George can stay with Lady Marshall." She went up to the couch and looked down at the white-faced woman looking up at her. "I've arranged for you to go to the private floor. I'm sure that's what you want, isn't it?"

Lady Marshall nodded. "Yes, of course," she said quickly. "I'd rather not be in a big ward."

"I thought that, and I've rung the senior surgeon to come in and look after you." She pressed Lady Marshall's hand reassuringly. "Nurse will stay with you and take you up to the private ward. I'll come with you. I'll be back shortly."

Lady Marshall nodded thankfully and watched Marion Hughes's neat, retreating figure. She raised her eyes to the nurse standing beside her. "What a charming woman," she said. "How reassuring and efficient." The nurse nodded and smiled down at the patient but refrained from making any remark.

Marion Hughes walked out of the Casualty department with a determined step. She would go up to the private ward and see that the room was properly prepared for Lady Marshall, then come back to Casualty and help convey her up there. As she walked along the corridor and turned to go up the stairs, she felt an unusual stab of nervousness. In her ability to handle the situation as far as the patient, the theatre, and the ward were concerned, she had no doubts, but as to her ability to handle it as a woman and make Sir James think of her as desirable, she was not so sure.

There was one thing she must do though. She hurried upstairs to her office, lifted her phone, and asked for an outside number, automatically looking at her watch at the same time. She hoped Mr. Mayes hadn't gone to bed.

"Mayes here." His voice sounded cheerful and wide awake over the phone.

"This is the night superintendent of St. Jude's. I hope I haven't got you up, Mr. Mayes."

"No, I was reading, just thinking of going to bed. What's up?" His voice sounded amiable.

"Well, Miss Creasey, the night casualty officer, has made a mistake. She misread the list, and—er—we've got an R.T.A. in, abdominal injuries, and she's called Sir James. I have rung him back, to try to stop him coming, but unfortunately he'd already left."

"That was a bit stupid of her, wasn't it? I should think the lists are plain enough." Gordon Mayes's voice still sounded amiable; he was an easy-going fellow.

"Well . . . it was just one of those things. Miss Creasey doesn't always . . . but I mustn't say that of course." Miss Hughes made her voice light and warm. "We all make mistakes sometimes, don't we?"

"Yes, sure, but I should have thought . . . Well, never mind. If Sir James is annoyed about it, tell him that I'll do a call for him when he's on. O.K.?"

"That's nice of you, Mr. Mayes," said Marion Hughes. "Nice of you to be so understanding. I'm sure Sir James will be equally so."

"I hope he'll have a word with Creasey, though," said Mayes, his voice becoming a little brisker.

"Oh, I'm sure he will," said Marion Hughes. "Good night, then, Mr. Mayes," and she put the phone back gently on its cradle.

Up in the operating-theatre they had been alerted and started the usual routine. The night theatre sister was making the appropriate calls: the senior anaesthetist, because it was Sir

James operating, and a fairly crucial op. at that; Nigel Denton to assist; private ward to see if they had been informed, and the night theatre porter. Double checks in St. Jude's were usually necessary.

The theatre light was switched on and shone down on the cushions on the operating table. The electric sterilizer was turned on, in case extra instruments were wanted in a hurry, though the abdominal trolley with its array of instruments would come soundlessly up from the sterilizing unit when it was summoned.

The night theatre sister went through to her own changing room to get into her theatre gear. A telephone rang. "This is Miss Hughes, Sister. I'll be scrubbing for Sir James."

There was a moment's stunned silence. "May I ask why?" the night theatre sister said.

"Yes, you may ask why. This is an important case, and you know my theatre experience is as wide as yours, and I mean to keep it fresh. Therefore I shall be scrubbing."

"But Miss Hughes . . ." The enraged theatre sister could hardly speak. But the phone at the other end had been put down and she was left, left with the receiver in her hand and a look of blank fury on her face.

"That woman," she muttered to herself. "I suppose I'd better run for them. What the hell does she want of him? What's happening? She's up to something."

She went on changing into her theatre clothes. This would mean she would be runner, a junior position for a theatre sister, but she'd rather do that than leave her theatre altogether. She came out of the office and informed one of her two nurses that she would be running. They looked at her with the astonishment she had felt.

"Miss Hughes will be scrub nurse," she said. "So you'd better look out, both of you, and see that the place is run efficiently."

"It always is, Sister," said one nurse rather pertly, and the night theatre sister's heart went out to her.

"I know that." She hesitated to say any more. After all, for one senior nurse to speak of another in a derogatory way just wasn't done, so she kept her mouth shut. She felt by her quickened pulse and the anger in her that she would have great difficulty in controlling her attitude to Miss Hughes when she eventually arrived in the theatre.

It came down the grapevine to Hiram Jones that a case had come in, that Miss Hughes had taken it over entirely, offending casualty sister, outraging the night theatre sister, and was going to scrub up for Sir James, who was not even the surgeon on call.

That would mean, Hiram thought, that she would miss the two o'clock round. Thank God, he thought, a bit of peace, and decided to go down to the kitchen for some potatoes and make himself a fry-up, at least he could do that. Today had been terrible.

The chances of getting drugs were lessening. The old men were fractious if they didn't get them, and one had complained to Miss Hughes—that old devil Machin, of course. If ever a bell rang in the night, it was Machin; if ever a moan went out to Miss Hughes about not having a wink of sleep, it was Machin; and it was Machin who unsettled the others. He'd sworn to her last night, or rather yesterday morning, that he hadn't had his sleeping pills, and Hiram had said defensively, "He doesn't always remember. His memory is a little defective."

Old Machin had heard him and called out, "Not as defective as yours. You never gave 'em to me. I know when I've had 'em, Miss."

Miss Hughes had given him a steady look as she said, "He's one of the few remaining old gentlemen on Nembutal, isn't he?" Hiram had nodded miserably and felt John would soon be without his pilly willies if he didn't find another way of getting them, other than taking them from patients.

At that moment the buzzer went in the ward, and again Hiram swore softly under his breath.

"Bet it's Machin," he muttered. It wasn't. It was another old man, right at the top of the ward.

"I've got a pain in me chest," he said, looking accusingly at Hiram.

Pain in the chest, that could not be ignored. Hiram Jones patted him reassuringly and said, "All right, where is it?" The old man made a motion with his withered hand, across his chest to his left arm. That was enough for Hiram. He padded softly down the ward, having switched off the old man's red light, and put on his blue night-light. Reaching the telephone, he dialled.

"Dr. Patel," he said. "I think you'd better come up and look at an old chap up here. He's got pains in his chest, going down his left arm, he's eighty, still . . ."

The Asian voice at the other end acquiesced. Hiram put the phone down, wheeled the E.C.G. machine towards the bed, and drew the curtains round it in case it should be needed. Well, there goes me fry-up, he thought.

In the children's ward Nurse Carmichael had also heard the news; it doesn't take long in a hospital. During her free hour she had been told the lot by a goggling nurse, who made it sound worse than it was.

"There was a terrible row; it was awful, I believe. You could hear them right down the corridor, Creasey and old Hughes, you know what they're like," and so on and so on. It had been a nice break in the night, and Nurse Carmichael had eaten it up.

It meant the same to her as it did to Hiram: no two o'clock round. Bliss. She'd be able to sit there quietly, if none of her little bastards started crying. She went back to the ward after her break feeling happier than she had done for nights. She even smiled at her junior as she sent her off for her break.

"Any trouble?" she asked.

"No." Her junior snatched up her cloak. "All the little kiddy winkies as quiet as little mice, but I can't vouch for them now that you've come back, love," and she gave the staff nurse a large wink and whisked off down the corridor.

Oh, to be like her, thought Carmichael; oh to be like that kid who doesn't give a damn whether she's ever going to be a sister, got innumerable boy-friends, would take a job in Woolworth's, doesn't care. If you're like that, you get on all right.

She sat down at her desk after she'd walked round all the little cages to see if everybody was quiet. The little asthmatic had gone home, so the night was no longer disturbed by his breathing. She'd no sooner sat down than she heard the familiar noise from the nursery, and then the wail. She sighed resignedly and walked down the ward into the nursery. The baby already had its mouth wide open ready to yell, when she picked it up. It was wet. She took off the napkin, dropped it into the pail beside the changing table, washed the child's bottom, and powdered it, the baby crying lustily the whole time.

When the child was changed and dry again, she held it in

her arms for a moment and looked down at it curiously. It
opened its rheumy eyes and looked at her. It had stopped
crying. It was a girl. As she looked at it, she wondered: would
it grow up to be a Nurse Carmichael, a Miss Marion Hughes?
God knows, she thought, but no feeling of fondness came
over her for the small bundle in her arms. Somehow Nurse
Carmichael always saw them as adults rather than babies. Vul-
nerable now, yes, but ready to grow up into something that
would bite your head off or do you an injury. Better to do
something to it now, she thought, before it could do any more
harm. The thought frightened her. She put the child hastily
back in the cot. It stayed quiet and went to sleep almost at
once.

George Hayward, asleep after a tiring day, was roused by the
phone ringing. "Bugger," he said loudly as he came awake. It
was Dr. Patel.

"I have a case here, on Stenton ward. Not quite sure about
it, doctor," he said. "He's got chest pains but . . . I wonder
if you'd come up and have a look at him."

George struggled up in bed.

"Why, for God's sake, can't you make up your mind again?
Are you sure it's not his appendix?" he said irritably, still full
of sleep.

Dr. Patel sounded apologetic but worried.

"O.K., O.K.," said George good-naturedly. "I'll come. Hold
your horses, don't do anything rash. I'll be there."

He was sorry for Patel. It must be murder working in a
country where even the language was difficult. He swung his
legs over the side of the bed, dragged his trousers up over his
pyjamas, and pulled a woolly over his head. He looked at the

little travelling clock by his bed: half-past one. Well, I should be able to decide and get back to bed again in an hour, he thought to himself.

He made his way from the doctors' house, across the garden, and looked down suddenly to notice he'd still got on his bedroom slippers. He hoped he didn't meet Marion Hughes. She looked you up and down and anything like that would be duly noticed with some charming little remark like, "Really doctor, can't you have things to hand ready for night calls?" Bloody woman.

He entered the hospital and started up the stairs towards the geriatric ward. He didn't use the lift; it wasn't encouraged at night. "The noise you know"—another little remark of Miss Hughes—"it disturbs the patients." That bloody woman runs the hospital, he thought to himself, and everybody in it.

Sir James Hatfield had gone to bed early, and he roused himself from an uneasy sleep when the phone rang by his bedside. Since his wife had died, it was he who had to answer it. She had always been the first to be roused by the buzzing phone, and she used to pick it up, then gently touch him and say, "Jimmy, the hospital wants you."

Then she would get out of bed and go downstairs and make him coffee. He missed her in a shadowy sort of way, but then she'd been a shadowy sort of woman. The prestige of his rise to senior consultancy, and then his knighthood, had sat uneasily on her shoulders. The entertaining, too, had been a tremendous nervous strain for her. He had known that; perhaps he'd never thanked her enough. Anyway, her death had been a shock.

He fumbled with the phone and eventually muttered into it, "Sir James Hatfield, yes?"

It was a nurse speaking. He bristled a little. What was a nurse doing ringing him?

"There's a case in Casualty, sir. Miss Hughes asked me to

ring you." The voice was apologetic, yet somehow sure of itself. It went on, "There's a Lady Marshall in Casualty, and Miss Hughes thinks it would be better if she went to the private floor. We have told the patient she must be admitted, and . . . she wishes to be private."

"What's the matter with her, nurse?" Sir James knew that he shouldn't ask the nurse, he should ask the doctor, but he was beginning to realize how this case had got to him. He knew, only too well, that in fact he wasn't the consultant surgeon on call. Miss Hughes must be manoeuvring.

"A ruptured spleen, Dr. Creasey thinks, sir."

"Right, thank you, nurse, I'll be there," said Sir James automatically. He put the phone back and for a moment rested his head on the headboard of the double bed.

Lady Marshall. He didn't know her, but a title always meant money. He wondered about Marion Hughes. How had she got round the fact that he wasn't the consultant on call? Well, he'd find out. She was obviously taking a chance that Lady Marshall had money, or perhaps she'd found out in some way that she had—her car, her clothes. Marion Hughes was clever enough, no doubt about it; but he'd been had this way before. Patients had ways of getting round paying; they had the operation in the general ward and then asked to be moved to the private floor. He knew their little tricks, every one of them.

He threw the bedclothes back and got out of bed. Well, he just hoped that Marion Hughes was not making a mistake. He didn't like being called in the middle of the night for something the new man, what was his name, Denton, could easily have coped with. He didn't like it at all, but if it meant a good, fat fee, well, he wasn't grumbling. He wondered about Marion Hughes. She had done this once before—was it before, or after, Lottie had died? He couldn't remember, but what was she after? He wondered.

He dressed quickly, yet without apparent speed. When he'd finished, the long mirror in his bedroom showed him from head to foot, the immaculate consultant surgeon, not one who had hurried out unshaven to the theatre: those days were gone. He stood looking at himself in the mirror and running the electric battery shaver round his chin. Then he went into the bathroom and put a couple of drops into his eyes to freshen them and take away the sleepy feeling; he pulled down his waistcoat decisively. He looked every inch the consultant, the very one to be called to operate on a Lady Marshall. She could be a baronet's wife, a knight's wife, a baronet's widow; a very wealthy woman, for all he knew. It was best to play it safe. He wondered again about Gordon Mayes, if someone could have made a mistake, or . . . But he'd leave that for the moment.

He switched off the bedroom light, went quickly downstairs, switching on the hall light, and, leaving it on, closed the front door and went round and pulled up the door of his garage. Inside, the Rover blinked at him reassuringly, reflecting the street lamp. He got in the car; one touch and it purred into life. Certainly it was a good buy, this car; he liked it, but he would prefer, and would later try and get, a Rolls. Oh well, maybe Lady Marshall would contribute to it. The car drew quietly out into the street. He started off to St. Jude's.

Nigel Denton answered the phone in much the same way as the other two had done.

"O.K. I'll be there," he said sleepily. He, too, swung his legs out of bed and swore. No matter how many night calls you had, you didn't grow to like them. He wondered why Sir James was to be there for a ruptured spleen. He could easily handle it himself. Why should Sir James be called anyway, when the other surgeon should have been?

He had done the day's operating list with Sir James and had not been particularly impressed with his surgery. It was adequate but not brilliant. He felt there was little to be learned from him. However, as he dressed hastily, he thought it was probably a private patient. He had no illusions as to why Sir James should turn up for a perfectly normal operation and call him out too. He would have to assist, that was that. He wondered if Sir James paid his assistants; he wondered, too, if he'd brush up against Marion Hughes—hardly likely in the operating theatre.

He pulled his clothes on, a woollen pullover and a pair of jeans left at the side of the bed for this purpose, zipped himself up, shivering slightly in the cold night air. He let himself out of the doctors' house and went across the lawns towards the hospital.

He looked up at it and at the various lights; at the big theatre window reflecting light across the garden, the small light next to it, coming from the recovery room; a light in one of the wards, where was that? He tried to place it. Men's geriatric; might mean George was up too. Well . . .

He shrugged himself further into his polo-necked woolly and pushed open the doors of the hospital, grateful for the warmth that greeted him. That was one thing: hospitals were always pretty warm to come into on a cold night.

Sir James drove into the hospital entrance and parked in the space marked with his name. It gratified him, that space, in spite of the fact that he had been driving his car into it for years. He got out, locked the car, walked into the hospital, acknowledging the deferential "Good evening, sir," from the telephone operator. He ran lithely up the stairs towards the theatres. He knew the embargo on lifts put on by Miss Hughes and normally would have taken no notice and used one, but tonight he felt he owed her a little, so he took the stairs and arrived at the top, to his satisfaction, without a shade of breathlessness. He looked up and saw the lights above the door, OPERATION IN PROGRESS, pushed through and opened the theatre doors.

The table was already in position. The theatre lights were lit, the trolleys grouped around, covered with their green, sterile towels, two nurses visible. He closed the door and went into the changing room. Nigel Denton's clothes were draped across a chair; he must be here already. He nodded to himself, that was satisfactory; he liked to be the last person to make an entrance. He changed into his theatre garb and walked through into the scrubbing-up area. Denton was scrubbing there already, and he turned to him and said, "Good evening, sir," through his mask.

Sir James nodded briefly, then turned to greet the night sister scrubbing beside him. Blue eyes he knew well met his over the mask.

"Good evening, Sir James," Miss Hughes said smoothly. "I thought as you were coming in, I'd scrub up myself."

"That's extremely gratifying, Miss Hughes," said Sir James with pleasure. "I know the famous surgeons you have worked for. I'll certainly do my best not to let you find them better than I am myself." He gave a comradely laugh and got into his mask.

As Marion Hughes went on scrubbing she murmured, "There's little fear of that, I'm sure, Sir James."

Nigel made a face behind his mask. He had been startled when he arrived at the theatre to find that Marion Hughes was there, and had asked the night sister why she was merely acting as a runner and Marion Hughes was scrubbing up, and her reply—"Don't ask me, ask that bitch. She's up to something"—had startled him a little.

He looked curiously past Sir James, along at the bowed head, with the theatre cap almost concealing the dark lustrous hair. He remembered his first day, when she'd walked down the steps, and he'd wondered who she was. Well . . . he knew now. He wondered, too, who the famous surgeons were for whom she had worked, and why she had taken it upon herself to scrub for Sir James tonight. He thought she wouldn't do anything unless it was for a good reason. Private patient? He supposed there might be a fee involved, but she didn't appear to him to be the type of woman who would worry about money. He dismissed the thoughts and got on with his scrubbing. Soon they all three walked into the theatre, to the patient, lying already anaesthetized, waiting, on the theatre table.

The senior anaesthetist, Dr. Galbraith, whom Nigel had met before during the day list, was seated at the head of the table. The patient was intubated, deeply unconscious, and ready for the knife that was handed immediately by Denton to Sir James.

Sir James looked at the anaesthetist, who nodded. Denton swabbed the exposed area, which gleamed white among the green towels, and Sir James cut down.

In Denton's opinion the incision was slightly larger than was necessary for a splenectomy, but as the operation proceeded, Denton noticed the efficiency with which Marion Hughes worked in concert with Sir James Hatfield; once his hand was held out, the required instrument would be slapped into it immediately. She obviously knew exactly how Sir James worked.

The nurse wheeled the swab rack to the end of the table, and the bloodied swabs started to be hung up as the operation continued, so that the count could be checked at the end of the operation.

Sir James chatted amicably as he worked. "Oh dear, ruptured indeed. Look at this, Denton. Not much use to her any more. Care for a look, Galbraith?"

The anaesthetist rose, came and looked at the mass of blood and tissue being removed from the incision—drawn back into a wide, deep hole by the retractors. He nodded, then went back, and became again deeply immersed in his copy of the *British Medical Journal*. He looked up now and again and checked his anaesthetic machine, then his nose went back into the book. Suddenly . . .

"Rather blue, old boy," said Sir James. Dr. Galbraith looked up, startled.

"Sorry," he said and gave the patient a little more oxygen. Sir James nodded in approval. It was a composed, ordinary scene. Denton felt that Lady Marshall would have a rather longer scar on her abdomen than was entirely necessary, but otherwise she would be all right. He was left to put in the last sutures and did so neatly and deftly. Marion Hughes dabbed the incision with a swab, threw it onto the trolley, and slipped off her gloves. She took from the waiting nurse the long strip of plaster to cover the wound and put it on quickly, competently, then dried round the plaster with another swab. The operation was over. Their eyes met as she did so. She pulled down her mask and smiled and said just loud enough for Sir James to hear, "A beautifully performed operation, Mr. Denton. It's a pleasure to assist Sir James."

Denton looked over at the great man. It was obvious that he had heard; a slight alteration in his stance showed it. Nothing more was said, Denton did not answer her.

The nurses removed the towels. The blanket was put on, the theatre porter was called, the patient gently transferred from table to trolley and taken back to the private ward.

Well, he was aware that the whole thing had been a ma-
noeuvre. Gordon Mayes should have done the operation and
probably received the private patient fee. But however it had
been worked, the patient had been operated on satisfactorily
and that, thought Denton, was the most important thing.

Sometimes, he thought grimly, one cannot hear the cries of
the patient for the sound of grinding axes.

Sir James, Nigel Denton, and Miss Hughes walked out of the
theatre, leaving behind them the nurses to clear up; to send
the instruments down for resterilization, put the dirty towels
down the linen chute, clean the theatre, do everything that
had to be done after an operation, night or day.

Marion Hughes pulled off her theatre cap. Her hair fell
luxuriously down her back and round her face; it was long, and
because of being continually curled into a bun at the nape of
her neck, now curled softly at the ends and bounced a little as
she walked. Nigel looked at her as they went towards the
theatre duty room and thought, she's a good-looking woman,
pity she's such a bitch. Sir James, who was looking at her too,
thought much the same, though he was less conscious how
her bitchiness had affected the hospital.

Marion Hughes made it obvious as she turned to Sir James
that she was addressing him only and not Nigel. "There's
some hot coffee in the duty room, Sir James," she said. "Do
come through and I'll get them to bring Lady Marshall's
notes in. Then you can write them up in comfort."

Sir James nodded. He didn't want to go into the duty room,
but on the other hand the operation notes might just as well
be written up now, and as she was a private patient he preferred to do it himself rather than leaving it to his registrar.

He nodded in dismissal to Nigel, who turned off into the changing room, and followed Marion Hughes into the duty room.

"I don't think I need any coffee, Miss Hughes. If I drink coffee now, I won't sleep for what is left of the night. It's all right before an operation but not afterwards." He sat down rather heavily at the desk and said almost irritably, "Where are the notes, then? Let me get on with it and write them up."

A nurse appeared with a buff folder containing Lady Marshall's notes.

"Here they are, Sir James," Marion Hughes said and put them down in front of him on the desk. "Are you sure you won't have coffee?" she asked again.

"Well, is there any hot milk?" Sir James asked. "I'd rather have more milk than coffee."

"Certainly." Marion Hughes poured milk and a dash of coffee into a cup and put it at his elbow, then poured one for herself. She sat down opposite him, on the other side of the desk, watching as he wrote in his scribbly doctor's handwriting describing the operation he had performed on the patient, what he had found, and the future treatment he recommended.

Marion Hughes waited as his pen scratched busily on, and then suddenly said, "Should the ward sister give her some penicillin before she comes round?"

Sir James looked up in surprise. It was not the night superintendent's job to suggest what drugs the patient should be given, but as he met those pale blue eyes and saw in them an expression he didn't quite understand, he said rather lamely, "Yes, a good idea. One can't be too careful—I'll do that."

He continued to write, and Marion Hughes continued to watch him. As she did so, she put her hand up and furtively pulled the soft brown hair farther round her face. She felt her heart beating faster than usual. She was nervous. She had got to try now to do what the young nurses did so easily. She had got to try and make herself appear attractive, desirable—what was the word—bedworthy—to Sir James. After all, she was well aware that he wouldn't think of marriage for at least a year, but it needn't start with marriage, it could start with an affair. If only, she felt, she were more confident and knew something to say that would arouse in him at least a feeling of interest. But while he went on writing she said nothing.

When his pen stopped, he capped it and put it into his inside pocket; she at last spoke. "Sir James, it is very nice to see you. I don't see enough of you on night duty, it's one of the disadvantages . . ." She lowered her head a little and looked up at him through her lashes, trying to make a half smile play round her nervous mouth.

Sir James looked up, his face startled. Good God, she's trying to flirt with me, he thought. Well, we must put a stop to that. He paused for a moment and looked at the face in front of him. With her hair falling provocatively she looked quite different but did not attract him in the least. He dropped his eyes, and his hands moved up and down the buff folder on the desk.

"Come, come. I do quite enough night calls as it is and certainly don't wish to do more. I can't quite understand how I got this one. After all, Gordon Mayes should have been called, shouldn't he?" His eyes, as cold as hers, appraised her.

Marion Hughes lost her head. "I thought as it was a private patient . . . You usually are very pleased to get them, Sir James," she said, but knew that the remark antagonized him.

"I'm not that fond of money, Miss Hughes, I assure you," he said. "Please don't do this again. If Gordon Mayes is on call, he's on call, and I don't wish to come out whether the patient is private or public."

It was a rebuff, the thing Marion Hughes dreaded more

than anything else, a rebuff. She had lost; she had been clumsy. She couldn't even emulate those young nurses with their downcast eyes or their direct flirtation. She couldn't do it. With men she was a failure, but she had something else up her sleeve, and his rebuff, and the stinging pain she felt from it, caused her to use it.

"I don't know how you're going to excuse this—" Sir James stopped, obviously at a loss for a word, and then went on— "excuse this lapse of memory that everyone seems to have had about the name on the list, if, of course, it was a lapse of memory and not a deliberate effort to throw this private patient my way. You haven't known me long, Miss Hughes, but you should have known me better than that."

"I have known you longer than you think, Sir James," Marion Hughes said. "I knew you when you were house physician at Manton Hall Hospital." She turned and waited for the effect on him; it was instant.

"Manton Hall, you knew me at Manton Hall?" Sir James's face was startled, much more startled than he had been when she had attempted to flirt with him.

"Yes indeed. I was a cadet then, seventeen. They put you on the children's ward, but you see things, you listen, you take it in amazingly well, and you remember it. One is very impressionable at that age, Sir James."

She turned away from him, her arm still uplifted finishing off the neat arrangement of her hair, no longer coquettishly around her face, back in its usual neat position—she was the night superintendent again. The reflection in the mirror gave her back a little of her confidence but took away none of her resentment.

Sir James continued to stare at her for a second or two more, then dropped his eyes. "Will you be kind enough to get a nurse to take these notes up to the private floor, please," he said, his voice lower, more subdued—thoughtful.

Marion Hughes felt a great desire to smile broadly but restrained herself. "Certainly, Sir James. I won't trouble to call a nurse. I'll take them up for you myself." She picked up the buff envelope, which he had put down again on the desk, and, as she did so, a whiff of her perfume reached him. It was repugnant to him. She carried the notes to the door, then turned and allowed herself a bright, cool smile.

"Good night, Sir James," she said. "Or should it be good morning?" She turned on her heel and left him, and he heard her walking softly along the corridor, towards the stairs that led down to the private ward.

Manton Hall, of all the coincidences, Manton Hall. He suddenly felt old. Then he braced back his shoulders with an effort, went across and took his coat from the hanger, and shrugged it on. He turned back to the desk, as if he'd forgotten something, but there was nothing there.

At that moment the night theatre sister walked into the theatre duty room. She had recovered her usual good temper and smiled at him.

"Not gone yet, Sir James?" she said. "Have the notes gone up to the ward?"

"What? . . . Oh, the notes. Yes, Miss Hughes has just taken them up herself."

The theatre sister looked at him. "Are you all right, Sir James?" she asked. Sir James nodded, then suddenly realized that he would rather be gone before Marion Hughes came back.

"Yes, I'm all right, thank you, Sister," he said evenly. "I was just going. Good night."

"Good night," the theatre sister said. And Sir James walked out of the theatre duty room and made his way down the stairs, through the front hall, out of the front entrance, and got into his car, but for a moment or two before he started it up, he sat there, thinking.

Nigel Denton left the theatre, walking behind Sir James and
Marion Hughes. The air prickled with her desire to be alone
with the great man, and Nigel felt no wish to thwart her in
this. As they moved towards the theatre duty room Nigel
turned aside into the changing room, feeling relief that he
could now get back to bed.

He pulled off his theatre gown and hat and mask and threw
them down on a chair, climbed back into his jeans and pullover, and walked out of the changing room. As he walked past
the duty room, into which Marion Hughes and Sir James had
retreated, he noticed the door was only half shut, so he called
out a soft good night. There was no reply, but he could hear
the murmur of their voices and wondered idly what they were
talking about. He ran down the three flights of stairs to the
front door, into the cold early morning.

He looked about him and thought that soon it would be
dawn, and grey streets would appear around St. Jude's, and
the birds would start twittering. Suddenly he felt wide awake
and the familiar need for a drink attacked him savagely. He
opened the doctors' house door and went up to his bedroom.
He thanked God that he'd had the sense to buy half a bottle
of whisky. He sat down on the side of the bed and debated
whether to have a drink or not. These were testing times.
Morning was near and his mind after operating seemed to
have become more alert. He wanted to think; the impressions
that had crowded in on him during his first days in St. Jude's
jostled for position in his mind. Sir James Hatfield, Gordon
Mayes, June Fyldes, even the spotty little nurse in the theatre,
all seemed to be trooping round in his mind for him to think
about, sort out, assess.

The need for alcohol overcame him, not to stimulate him, but to soothe him. He got up, went over and put his hand in his coat pocket, and drew out the half bottle of whisky. He held it in the palm of his hand, idly reading the label, then went over and picked up his tooth mug and poured out a generous measure, screwed the cap back on the bottle, telling himself that that was it, a nightcap, no more. He lay on the rumpled bed, bunching the pillows behind his head, and sipped the whisky. It warmed him and made him feel better immediately; though the depression that had descended on him like a cloak in the hospital stayed with him. But it was better; life almost became bearable again with a drink in your hand. It seemed it wasn't the effect of the drink but the feeling of safety, the warmth, the very handling of a glass with alcohol in it; that didn't stop him getting drunk, though, he thought. He glanced sideways at the other bed; many of the registrars were married, so the quarters had to be suitable for husband and wife. The empty bed, neat, covered with a flow-ered counterpane, brought back such a flood of memories, such an overwhelming sense of guilt and shame and horror, that he got up again, refilled the tooth mug, and brought it back. He sat on the bed, this time his back firmly towards its twin.

He thought of his wife, as he knew he would. He had to fight this memory: that was what his friend, the psychiatrist, had said, when he talked to him about this recurring, waking nightmare. He had got to put it out of his mind. You can't do anything about it; regret won't help. He had repeated this to himself a thousand times. But once the memory started up he could never, never, stop it; he had to go through the whole thing, like a movie that had to be run, like a soundtrack that had to be played back. That was why he drank, he told himself, that was why he drank.

The movie in his mind began where it always did. He had

been young when he married, just qualified. His wife was young too, eager, full of life. He'd met her in a night-club—she was a stripper. He loved her. What she did was just a job, something that could be stopped the moment they were married. He didn't want other men looking at her naked. For a year it had seemed it would work.

Then Mandy had grown restless; the old life had far more pull than Nigel was able to understand, or so Mandy said. She'd got to go back to it. He hated the idea of what she wanted to do, but she loved the life, the excitement, the music, the dancing, and the drinking; it added the vital warmth and the kicks to her life. She had said to him so many times that she couldn't stand suburban life. The quarrels got fiercer, the drinking got more frequent and more serious, and her drinking spread to him. He took a drink and they were quarrelling; she took one too, and they both became drunk and more and more quarrelsome, more and more violent.

The movie reeled on in front of his memory's eye. The soundtrack played accurately and minutely as if it were in the room and not inside his head.

Nigel had awakened one night about three A.M. Mandy wasn't home. It wasn't unusual, but this night, suddenly, he was filled with such hatred of the life she was living—or was it of Mandy herself?—and the kind of life they were trying to live together that he had got up, pulled on some clothes, gone to the garage, determined to go to the club and drag her out and say, "This is it, no more!" Why this urge should come to him so suddenly he couldn't remember. It was as if he had been awakened from a nightmare about her or from dreaming of her.

The night had been misty and cold. He remembered banging the front door, opening the garage, getting into the car, and starting up the engine. It started reluctantly. It was an old car, and it jerked backwards out of the garage. He knew from experience the quick reverse down the short drive, out through the gate. Only once had he grazed the car slightly, and that was when they first moved into the house. He backed the car quickly down the drive, across the path, and out into the road. There had been a sudden sickening bump.

Nigel held his head in one hand and then drank a little more deeply from the whisky. There was very little left now of the whisky or the memory; the movie had nearly run its full course. He had stopped the car, got out. There, half under it, with a leg under one wheel, lay Mandy. A great gash across her forehead was bleeding freely. He didn't need to be a doctor to know she was dead. The ambulance, the police, the test to see if he'd been drinking. It was negative of course; he hadn't been drinking, he'd been sleeping.

The story, first in the local paper, then in the nationals. He had told the reporters that he had been going to fetch his wife from the club. Why on this particular night? He hadn't been able to say. Just that it was such a cold, dreary night, he thought it would be nice for her to have him fetch her. It sounded right; there was no Mandy to tell it any other way.

Nigel was drunk now. He felt warm and comforted, he had got all the way through the horror; it would go away now for a while, he knew this. Why it came flooding back suddenly he didn't always know. Maybe the twin bed had triggered it off this time. Sometimes it could be someone who looked like Mandy. Often, if he was called in the night it happened. Well, it was over. He'd got to make his future and this drinking had got to stop; there would be no more. He wouldn't even buy another bottle, he thought muzzily as he leaned back on the pillows, but he wasn't so drunk that he didn't realize, as he always did, how easy it was to say no more when you were full of booze. It was like cigarettes: so easy to say that you wouldn't buy another packet if you had a full packet in your pocket. He fell asleep.

On the children's ward Nurse Carmichael was having a more restful night. She looked at the ward clock: half-past four. Miss Hughes had missed the two o'clock round; it had been done by the junior night superintendent, who made no demands, no sarcastic asides. Even the junior nurse felt better for it and was in the kitchen cooking tea for them. It was strictly against the rules, but they had at least three hours with no Miss Hughes. It was wonderful.

Carmichael smelled appreciatively the aroma of chips, made from potatoes begged from Mrs. Upton, coming from the kitchen. Egg and chips, delicious for night-time tea. She looked forward to it and her long nose twitched, not this time with anxiety, but with anticipation.

The babies were quiet in the nursery as she went round looking at them. On a night like this you felt fonder of the children. It was only that bitch Hughes who made you so edgy with them.

Carmichael went back into the ward, sat down at the desk, and started to fill in her report sheet. She knew what had kept Miss Hughes away of course—Sir James and the operation. Trust Miss Hughes to suck up to Sir James; wonder what she's up to? Wouldn't be surprised if she's after him.

If only Sir James would marry Marion Hughes; that would mean that someone else would get the job, it couldn't be any worse. Then she herself might become sister . . . Carmichael shook herself. This was just dreaming. Sir James wouldn't look at anybody for another year at least, and by that time the post on the women's surgical ward would be filled, and Nurse Carmichael would still be Nurse Carmichael.

She felt a great surge of bitterness and boredom at the

thought of going back to her bed-sitting room. Somehow the little bit of freedom tonight had made her feel that the possibility of getting some better post wasn't so far away; then the bed-sitter would be no more, it would be a nice flat as she was sure Miss Hughes had. The extra money would make all the difference. She could furnish it and . . . It had been this stint of night duty that had made such inroads into her confidence. She jabbed the pen angrily into the paper on which she was writing. No woman should bring as much unhappiness into a place as this woman does, she thought. The people she'd reported. Dear old Jones on the geriatric ward, he'd been up on a complaint, in front of the Committee, because of Miss Hughes. He'd nearly lost his job. She couldn't remember what it was about, ill-treating one of the old men? She didn't think so but couldn't remember.

Then there was the night cook, the one before Mrs. Upton. She'd been chucked out because Miss Hughes said she'd found her stealing food. She had too, but it was only the remains she'd been taking out, the remains of an awful chicken meal they'd had in the middle of the night. She had said it was for her cat or her dog, but Miss Hughes hadn't listened; she'd reported her, and she'd got the sack. There was no end to the harm Miss Hughes could do. Why? Carmichael wondered. Why was she always on the look-out for something to report? She supposed to make herself look more efficient. There was the Creasey scandal and that man with the angina. There was one thing after another . . .

Her junior nurse interrupted her thoughts. "Meal's ready," she said softly from the door. Nurse Carmichael put up her hand and frowned and looked round the ward but nobody had wakened. She got up and went to the kitchen for the illicit egg and chips.

"Better see the smell's gone before the morning round," she said, sitting down at the table in front of the plate full of chips and the gleaming, sunlike egg. The junior, her own plate in front of her, sat down opposite her. "Lovely," she said.

Nurse Carmichael nodded. She was just about to cut into the egg, let the yolk run over her chips, when she looked up— there in the doorway stood Miss Hughes.

Hiram Jones, in spite of the fact that Miss Hughes had missed a round, was having a hell of a night. John had been particularly difficult all day, mostly because there had been no pills for him in the morning. Tonight Hiram had decided that he'd got to take home at least six Nembutals. There were very few Nembutal capsules given out now, and there were no new ones being recommended by the doctors. They were trying to get those old men who'd been on them for years off them and on to less addictive drugs, but some of the old boys just wouldn't settle unless they had their familiar capsules; and so a few were ordered still.

This evening Hirma had managed to hold back six. The three men who should have had them were sleepless and demanding, and the red lights above their beds went on frequently as they used their buzzers. One did now.

Hiram padded up the ward, right to the end. It was old Mr. Butterworth, a Nembutal taker, who'd been denied his because of John.

"I haven't had a wink of sleep all night," he said. "I'm going to report it to someone or other. Look, it's nearly five o'clock, and I haven't slept a wink. You know that, I've kept on telling you, and I didn't have my pills, I can't sleep without 'em. Why won't you give 'em me? The doctor said . . ."

"Shut up," said Hiram. "You'll wake everybody up and then they'll all be buzzing and coughing and carrying on."

"Well, serve you right," said Mr. Butterworth. "Serve you damn well right. I should have had me pills. Why won't you give me them? I asked that young doctor when he came round yesterday morning, and he said I could have 'em, he said I could have my Nembutal. Why won't you give 'em me?"

"I did give them to you. You had them at ten o'clock. Shut up for goodness' sake," said Hiram.

"No, I didn't," said Mr. Butterworth. "I did not have them, you can say what you like. When Miss Hughes comes round I'm going to tell her I didn't have them, and it's no use you saying to her—I know what you say."

"I don't say anything," said Hiram wearily.

"Yes, you do. You say, 'They don't remember'; you say, 'They're senile, demented.' I know, I hate you," the old man said hysterically. "I'll get me pills somehow. They'll have to bring them for me from home. I'll make them. I've got some at home."

Hiram stopped in his tracks. "Have you?" he said, coming back to the bedside.

"Yes, I've got a whole bottle. I got them before the doctor knew I was coming into hospital, and I'm going to get my daughter to bring them in. I can keep them in my locker, and I won't have to rely on you." Suddenly his eyes went sly, and he said, "I shouldn't have told you. I should have got them and put them in my locker and said nothing, but I shan't tell you where I put 'em. No."

"Yes, you do that, you get that bottle from home," said Hiram. "You'd be very sensible if you had a bottle here. You could take two at night when I can't get them from the doctor; or if I'm not allowed to give them to you, then you can take two from your bottle. You get your daughter to bring them in."

Mr. Butterworth looked surprised at the amount of co-operation he was getting from the staff nurse. "Will you let me

phone her? It's visiting day," he said. "Will you bring me the
mobile phone, early, before she goes to work, when Miss
Hughes has done her round, like about eight o'clock?"

"Yes, I will," answered Hiram, trying to keep the eagerness
out of his voice. A whole bottle of the stuff, there might be
fifty or a hundred. I can take some and that will ease matters.
John likes Nembutal better than anything. It was a wonderful
idea.

"All right, I'll bring you the phone at eight. Remind me if I
forget, for you know how busy it is then," he said.

Mr. Butterworth nodded slyly. He liked Hiram Jones in
spite of the fact that he didn't always get his pills, and if he
would let him have them, a whole bottle in his locker, that
would be perfect.

Hiram went on round the ward, answering the buzzers that
Mr. Butterworth's talking had occasioned. He felt more lighthearted. If it worked, if the old man got that bottle into the
hospital, that would be something worth having. He'd take
them away from him of course on some pretext, take half of
them home.

John, John, John, beloved, he thought, I'd do anything for
you, steal, anything. I wonder if you'd do as much for me?

Marion Hughes was back in her office. It was quarter to five,
her tea-tray was on the table in front of her, later than usual,
but it had been worth it, worth letting her deputy do the
middle round. She still tingled with anger at Sir James
Hatfield's apparent immunity to her femininity. Well, the
words "Manton Hall Hospital" made him realize that she was
not to be swept aside so easily. She felt a sudden buildup of
confidence. What was it her mother used to say? She searched

her memory. "There are other ways of killing a cat than choking it with cream." Yes, that was right, quite a clever saying. She'd never appreciated it before.

She looked at her watch, nearly five o'clock; three hours and she'd have practically finished the night's stint. Two more nights, and then . . . nights off.

She walked over to the mirror. A touch more eye-shadow, she thought. Then, grimacing a little at her own reflection, she felt that he'd be getting quite a good bargain even if she did manage to blackmail him into marrying her. She remembered a party she'd been asked to some time ago at the Hatfields'. Lady Hatfield had looked dreadful, a lacquered hair-style—well really! She looked at herself again in the mirror. He'd be getting something better than that, even if, at the moment, he showed little appreciation of it.

It had been amusing to go down to the children's ward. Why had she done it? Just on impulse; it wasn't round time or anything. It was then you caught people doing things they shouldn't. Carmichael's face as she had looked up from the plate of egg and chips had really been worth seeing. That girl was a fool; the little junior nurse too, who'd cooked the meal. Well, she didn't think she'd say too much about her. Of course she'd done wrong to cook it, but then what could the child do? Miss Hughes smiled. Carmichael detested her, she knew. It would give her some satisfaction to report the small incident to the children's ward sister.

How did the fools think they could get away with it? Hiram Jones and his pill-pinching, Carmichael and her illicit meal. She supposed that Carmichael would have thrown all the windows up in the kitchen and frozen the place to get rid of the smell before she, Marion Hughes, came round; it really was most amusing. And that girl on the surgical ward, did she actually think that the night superintendent didn't know that her boy-friend, who was on duty too over on the telephone exchange, did she really think that the superintendent didn't know that he slipped over for tea at six in the morning? They were funny, hospital people. In some ways clever and astute when it came to diagnosing a patient's ailments, or telling the doctor symptoms, but in many ways so stupid. Yes, she would like to be Lady Hatfield, and there was plenty of time. She wondered as she poured out a cup of tea just exactly what Sir James was feeling.

John came into the flat about three in the morning. He was slightly drunk but no more, because he hadn't had the money for as many drinks as he'd wanted. His friends had got tired of treating him. He walked about restlessly, knowing that the amount of alcohol he'd had would stimulate him. He wouldn't be able to sleep. The only answer was pills.

He searched round the flat, looking in some of the pots where Hiram sometimes hid a couple of white capsules. He was a rotten sleeper and he just hoped that Hiram hadn't let him down. He searched almost frantically; he hadn't had any pills all day, but he could find nothing. Well, it was no good hanging about here. He'd do what he hadn't done before, go up to the hospital and see what the hell was going on. He looked at his watch: three o'clock. When did Hiram say that bitch did a round, two o'clock was it, and then seven in the morning? Something like that. It wouldn't take him long if he went on his motor bike. He'd be there in ten minutes.

He slid into his leather jacket again and picked up his crash helmet, then ran nimbly down the stairs, cursing to himself as he went. Why the hell couldn't they have a stock in the flat? Hiram working in a bloody hospital, you'd think at least . . .

He wondered sometimes whether he should go on with Hiram or find somebody else with a better supply.

He got on the bike and roared off into the night. As the air hit him, he felt slightly more drunk, steadied himself, and went slower. To be picked up by the police now, without a thing on him in the way of dope to take, that would be too much. He stopped outside the hospital, got off, and leaned the bike against the wall. He walked into the entrance hall. The telephone operator was dozing and didn't see him come through. It's quite peaceful, he thought, as he walked in, not a sound anywhere. He stood in the front hall, rather bewildered by the amount of notices, arrows pointing to X-ray, Casualty. Then he spied Stenton ward: that was what he wanted. As he made his way towards the stairs, a distinguished-looking man came down them and walked past him out of the front door, closing it quietly behind him. He looked preoccupied, worried. John turned and watched him get into a large car outside which he could just see in the dim light of the forecourt. He saw him sit there, in the car, not starting it.

"Nice," John said.

John had never been in the hospital before; he hated hospitals. It was only because he was desperate tonight that he'd come, that, and the fact that he'd had quite a bit of alcohol and wanted something to calm him down. If he didn't take something he'd be awake half the night.

Stenton ward. He followed the arrow and looked into the brightly lighted ward kitchen—no one.

He went to the door of the ward. He could see the rows of dim lights and a man coming towards him; it was not Hiram. He was a much younger boy, good-looking, and John wondered about Hiram and him, then dismissed the thought. Pills were more important than jealousy at the moment.

"Is Nurse Jones here?" he asked. The young male nurse looked at him curiously.

"No, but he's just due back from . . ."

"Rest? Ah."

The young nurse nodded. "I'm Atkins. The night superintendent's not due round yet, but it's a bit of an odd hour for visiting friends," he went on. He glanced at the watch pinned on the front of his white uniform, then up again at John, and smiled at him suggestively.

"Better wait in the kitchen. He won't be long. John is it?" He pushed open the kitchen door farther and sent a shaft of light streaming across the corridor. Someone in the ward coughed, a buzzer went.

"Bugger the old sods," said Atkins dispassionately. He turned away and disappeared back into the darkened ward.

John blinked in the light of the kitchen, sat down at the table, and drummed his fingers on the plastic surface. He hated this. He hadn't done it before, and he wouldn't do it again. As he'd stood at the ward door, his nose had wrinkled with distaste at the smell. A fusty smell, tinged with the smell of urine, food, and old bodies. He didn't like it at all and he didn't know how Hiram could stand it. Sometimes if he let himself think of Hiram doing things for these old men he could barely let him touch him, but well . . . Hiram was a good source of pilly willies, he thought, trying to be lighthearted and dismiss the feeling from his mind, but his imagination boggled at the thought of Hiram giving out the urinals and rubbing their backs . . . No, it didn't do to think about that. He got up and walked round the kitchen, whistling to himself tonelessly, and at that moment Hiram walked in.

"John, for God's sake, what are you doing here?" he said.

"I couldn't sleep. I've no pills. I'm sick of it," he answered. "I don't know whether it's any good being friends with someone who works in a hospital. I thought it was a good wheeze, but I don't know."

"And I thought you loved me," said Hiram, a trace of bitterness in his voice, but obviously trying to keep the scene undramatic. He noticed the petulant lower lip was stuck out as usual and the deprived look that John put on when he was wanting something and not getting it.

"Well, have you got anything? I've got to get something. I just want to get stoned, that's all."

Hiram put his hand in his pocket and took out two capsules.

"Is that all, for God's sake?" John raised his voice to a dangerous level, and Hiram resignedly fished in his pocket and gave him two more.

"That's all I've got," he said, "and the two old men I didn't give them to haven't slept a wink."

"Well, why can't you get some more?" John said. "I can't understand how anybody working in a hospital can't get more. Surely they don't count every bloody pill, I mean how can they? They couldn't keep up with it all."

"These they do," said Hiram. "They don't give many of these. There are others. I'll try and get you some, and I believe I'm going to be able to get some more of these, a bottleful."

"Well, that's better, if it's true, though God help you if I ever get on the hard stuff," John said.

"Don't talk like that, John, you know I couldn't. It would mean the sack. Just please cool it."

"Well," said John, "can't I have a cup of tea or something? Is it Ovaltine you drink in the night?" He giggled. "I met our young friend in there, Atkins, quite a looker. I hope you don't . . ."

"No, I don't," said Hiram tiredly. "You know I don't. I don't care for a soul but you."

"Better not, lovey," John simpered. "Well, I'll make do with these then. A chap passed me in the hall, good-looking, old though, distinguished. Rather my type, I thought."

"That would be Sir James Hatfield," said Hiram without interest. "He was in, doing a private case. Trust him, he wouldn't come in if it were an ordinary one."

"Don't blame him," said John. "I wouldn't work in this hole, only for money and lots of it, not for the pittance they give you." He flounced across the kitchen and turned at the door. "I'd better make myself scarce, hadn't I? Hughesie may be round, and that wouldn't do, would it? She wouldn't like that at all, though I'd love to see her. Don't forget to get some more, for God's sake." He held out his palm where the four capsules still lay, then he left.

Hiram gave a long sigh and walked into the ward to see what had happened while he had been away for his hour's rest. He hoped John wouldn't make a habit of coming to the hospital.

Sir James drove home slowly, thinking. He put the car away and let himself into the silent house. When Lottie had been alive, after a night call, she would be waiting up for him, fussing around making cocoa or some other obnoxious drink when he would have much preferred a whisky and soda. He went into the sitting-room and mixed himself one. It was a relief not to have her there. He had to think, he had to think hard. Manton Hall. What an awful, damned, stupid coincidence that that woman had been there when he had been there as house physician. What was she hinting at? What was she going to do with the knowledge he felt she must have?

The job of house physician at Manton Hall had been arduous, had tired him, young as he was: constant night calls, and then expected to work up to standard during the day. Everything about the hospital that he hadn't thought of for years came flooding back to him.

The children's ward, that's where one thing had happened. Was that what she knew about? In a way he hoped so. It was the lesser of two evils. It had been an accident, that child.

He had been called four times that night, and then to the children's ward at 3 A.M. for a meningitis; brought in uttering those strange, meningeal cries, the head tilted back, the neck stiff. It was easy to diagnose, he'd seen it before. He'd ordered intrathecal penicillin, penicillin straight into the spinal cord. He had been tired, dead tired. He could see the trolley now, laid up for the spinal tap, the nurse on the opposite side of the cot, waiting for him to tell her to position the child, and then her taking the small body and the feet and arching the child's body slightly over the edge of the bed. He scrubbed up, towelled the child except for the area on the small back bone where the needle was to be inserted, the nurse beside him swabbing the top of the bottle, plunging the needle in and drawing up the contents, his job, a million units instead of a thousand units of penicillin. Mixed by the nurse it was in those days, with sterile water. She had chosen the wrong bottle, and he had not read the label. Whose fault, the nurse's? For not showing him the label, for not tipping the bottle up and showing it to him as she was supposed to do? Whose fault, whose fault? The doctor is ultimately responsible for anything that goes wrong, but the nurse too in this case had been responsible. If only he had stuck to the rules and made her raise that bottle label to his eye level so that he could read it, but in the injection had gone.

The death of the child had been terrible for him. The parents had sued the hospital. There had been a Complaints Committee; the medical world had supported him wonderfully, and he had been exonerated. "Death by Misadventure," accidental death. Had it been an accident, though, or had it been negligence? They had decided but he had never really got over it.

By mentioning the name of that hospital, Marion Hughes had brought the whole thing back with such force that he tried to remember the face of that nurse who had held the bottle for him from which the penicillin had to be drawn, but he couldn't, it was a blank. He couldn't even remember her uniform, whether she was the staff nurse, or a junior nurse, nothing. Had she left, given it up? Poor kid, if she had gone through what he had gone through. Well, he supposed she had, but he couldn't remember what had happened to her. Indeed he had not thought of her to this day. Was that what Marion Hughes had been trying to remind him about, the death of that child? Or was it something worse, for there had been something worse at Manton Hall, something else—could she mean that? He got up restlessly. He couldn't sit still, he couldn't go to bed now. Did she know about the other thing, the abortion? Surely not; it had been so secret, so well done, and yet . . .

He had had an affair with a young nurse, eighteen. He could hardly remember her. It had been so transient, so passing. Some people said the nurses only came in to catch a doctor. Perhaps she had been trying to catch him, but anyway, he got her pregnant, and the one thing that he was determined about was that he'd never, never marry young, not until . . . Anyway, he'd given her £25 and told her to go and get rid of it. Vaguely her face came back to him, swollen with tears, puffy, not attractive. Why had he done it, what had he seen in her? Just a moment's incautious stupidity. She had gone on her night off to have the abortion and came back looking terrible. Three days later she was on the gynae ward. She had smuggled a note out to him, begging him to come and see her, but how could he? House physician visiting a nurse on a gynaecological ward? That would have looked strange, and he hadn't risked it, but he had spoken to the gynaecologist about it, casually, as if it were nothing to do with him, and the gynaecologist had told him about the case.

Been to some bloody outside abortionist, got retained products, septic, in a nice state. She could easily have died. I'd like to get hold of the bugger who made her pregnant and then sent her off like that. How would she know where to go? She's only eighteen. Of course she'd gone to some back-street woman instead of . . . he had gone on and on, and James Hatfield had realized just how tricky the situation was. If she told anybody, if she had mentioned his name, told them he'd given her £25 to go and get . . . had she? Had she been friends with Hughes, was it possible? That was bad, very bad. The other thing, well he had been exonerated, but the abortion, he wouldn't like that to come out, even at this late stage. Nobody knew, at least he'd thought nobody knew. He weighed it up in his mind. How should he handle this? He wasn't going to let that bitch bring up the child, that was bad enough; but if she knew the other thing, or both, she was a menace to him. Something had got to be done.

He remembered again the gossip about her reporting that —what was it?—angina case. He had got to find out what she knew. If it was the child, he could let it go, but if it was the abortion, the illegal abortion that he'd paid for, she'd have to be silenced somehow. Money? He didn't think much of that idea. He knew in the back of his mind what she wanted. Marriage. She wasn't young. Thirty-seven? Good-looking, but a cold fish.

Once Sir James killed a child; accidentally, so they said—he could ride that. But: once Sir James had an illegal abortion done on a kid, the girl nearly died, was brought into the hospital, I was there, she told me all about it—that was too much, that was too much. He was now free and eligible, and he wasn't going to marry a night superintendent. Madeleine, the

Honourable Madeleine Craughton, that was the one, that was
the one he was going to marry, who would grace his house and
table, yes, that was the one, and he'd see Marion Hughes in
hell before he'd let her stop him.

First, he must find out what she knew, what she wanted,
and then . . . He got up, feeling calmer, stood the whisky
glass back on the drinks cabinet, and went up to bed.

In the children's ward, Staff Nurse Carmichael was having a
rough ride. To be caught like that was the end. If only she
hadn't . . . She hadn't wanted the egg and chips all that
much, but to look up and find Marion Hughes standing there
with that smile on her face, that smug look, as much as to say,
"It's nothing more than I expected."

Carmichael had got to her feet, stammering as usual, feeling the grease of the chips round her mouth, not daring to get
a handkerchief out to wipe her face. "I'm so—so sorry, Miss
Hughes. I suddenly felt rather peckish, the night meal wasn't
very good, and I asked nurse if she'd . . ."

"Please don't go on, nurse, don't make excuses," Marion
Hughes had said coldly. "You know perfectly well you're not
supposed to cook on the ward, only the children's eggs in the
morning. I presume that two of their eggs have been used,
and as they are counted on the diet list, two children will be
short, or maybe you don't always put in quite the right
amount to Mrs. Upton for breakfast eggs. Perhaps you add
one or two more so that you and Nurse can regale yourselves.
It's stealing you know, stealing hospital property, you realize
that. Potatoes, too. Where did they come from? Begged from
Mrs. Upton, no doubt, very dignified from a staff nurse and a
would-be sister."

Nurse Carmichael had been silent. There was nothing she could say, nothing she could do. This woman was always the victor, and she was always the victim. It was better to be quiet. So she just stood there, and a sullen look came over her face that was unlike her, and Marion Hughes, she knew, had noted it. Carmichael could tell by the sudden stiffening of the figure at the door.

"Of course this will have to be reported to your day sister in the morning. There's nothing I can do about it. I like to protect my night staff and to keep them out of trouble, but it's so difficult when it contains people like you, Staff Nurse Carmichael. What kind of example is this to your young nurse? What do you think she'll do when she gets in charge of a ward? Where is she by the way?" she asked, looking at the deserted plate of egg and chips on the other side of the table. Nurse Carmichael nodded dumbly towards the ward. Just as her junior had been about to attack her meal, a child had cried out in the ward, and she had got up and gone to it. She would have the luck, thought Carmichael. Never me. Miss Hughes walked into the ward, leaving Nurse Carmichael alone in the kitchen.

She stood there, waiting. She knew the night super would reprimand the junior, but not as badly as she had her. After all, the junior was not responsible. Oh God . . .

When Miss Hughes and the nurse had walked out of the ward together, Carmichael had heard them from the kitchen.

"You should know better than that, Nurse. Of course, if your staff nurse asks you to do something, to cook for her, it's difficult for you. I'm glad to see you were in the ward. If anything like this happens again, please ring me and tell me that you find it impossible to do what your staff nurse is asking. Is that understood?"

"Yes, Miss Hughes," her junior had mumbled, and then Carmichael had heard Miss Hughes's footsteps walking away down the corridor. As her steps receded, the nurse had walked into the kitchen.

"Bloody hell," she had said. "All for a plate of soggy egg and chips. That woman wants doing."

"Stop using that language for goodness' sake. I don't like it." Nurse Carmichael had suddenly felt tears spring out of her eyes and the nurse had come over quickly and put her arm round her shoulders.

"Come on, Staff," she had said. "She's only a bloody superintendent, and I'm sorry about my language. I know I swear, but really she brings out the worst in me. As if I'd ring and tell her if you asked me to cook some egg and chips."

"It would be safer if you did," Carmichael had answered bitterly.

Hiram Jones had had the usual morning round, but if anything, Miss Hughes seemed in a lighter mood. In fact he had never known her quite so preoccupied, and preoccupation made her less critical.

"Good morning, Mr. Machin," she said. "Good morning, Mr. Johnson. I hope you've had a good night," and she had whisked by them rather quickly. The torn sheet that Hiram had seen hanging down by the side of one of the beds passed unnoticed. She had just circled the ward quickly and said, "Thank you, Nurse Jones," in her usual cold way and had gone. Hiram felt as if a great weight had lifted off his mind. The visit of John during the night had been bad enough. It was great to get a swift round done like this, almost without comment. He went to the kitchen where breakfast was being prepared and said, "I'm going to fetch the telephone."

"This early?" Atkins looked up in surprise.

"Yes, one of the old men wants to phone home; it's visiting day, remember, and he wants to ask his daughter to bring something in. It's important to do it early, she goes out to work. Did you see the telephone when you went on rest?"

"The telephone? Yes, I did, it's parked down by the lift. I'll get it if you like."

"No, get on with what you're doing, I'll get it," said Hiram. He didn't want his junior to hear any of the conversation that went on between the old man and his daughter. He wheeled the portable phone up the ward, its wheels making hardly any sound on the ward floor. He drew up at the old man's bedside.

"Mr. Butterworth," he said. Mr. Butterworth was dozing off again. "You wanted the phone, you know, to phone your daughter about your pills. Right?"

The old man opened startled, rheumy eyes and looked at him. "The what?"

"Your pills," said Hiram impatiently. "You remember, you said you wanted your pills, the bottle of Nembutal, at home."

"I had 'em last night," the old man said. "I had 'em last night. What are you talking about?"

"You said you'd like to have some in store, and you said you'd got a bottle at home and that your daughter would bring it in, remember? Then if the doctor won't let you have them, or if I can't give them to you because of the night superintendent, you know what I mean, you can have them in your locker and take them when you want."

"Ah, yes, I remember, that's right. Well I dunno," said the old man. Hiram was shaking with impatience.

"I would. Yes, I'd get them," said Hiram. He glanced round the ward. Thank God the old man in the next bed was deaf and hadn't got his hearing aid on, and the man in the other bed seemed to be asleep.

He plugged the mobile phone in and said, "What's the number? Have you got it?"

"I can't remember. She's my next of kin. It'll be in me folder, won't it?"

God, he's got a bit of sense left, thought Hiram Jones. He went to the file beside the desk, flipped through until he came to Mr. Butterworth, and there was the phone number of his daughter. Thank God she's on the phone, he thought, but then she would, wouldn't she? He had said so last night. But they are so muddled and confused. I just hope he's right and he's got pills there.

He went back to the bed and dialled the switchboard operator's office to ask for an outside line. He prayed she wouldn't listen to the conversation but remembered it was May on duty. He'd seen her when he came in last night; she was always half asleep, she wouldn't bother. He waited; the phone buzzed and buzzed. Because it was an interior call, May didn't bother all that much. It rang about ten times before she picked it up and in a sleepy voice said, "M-m?"

"I want an outside number for a patient." Hiram gave the number, and the red light came on on the mobile phone. Hiram waited a minute. He hoped she'd taken the headphones off. Then he dialled Mr. Butterworth's home number and handed the phone to the old man. "Go on, ask her. Say you want the bottle of Nembutal, go on," he said.

The old man took the phone, taking ages shifting up the bed, in order to get himself into a position where he could hold the receiver to his ear, and then he said, "That you, Mabel?"

A voice crackled back. "No, it's all right. I'm just phoning. Night staff said I could have the phone. I knew you'd be going to work in a minute. I want you to bring something this afternoon." The crackling on the other end of the phone continued. The old man held the phone away from his ear and raised his eyes to heaven, then put the receiver back to his ear.

"All right, it's nothing you've got to get. I know you haven't got much time. I just want you to bring that bottle of Nembutal out of the medicine cupboard in the bathroom. You know, it's got my name on it; it says—'Take one at night as required'—that's the one. The nurse here says I can have it. Well I know, but he does. If you want to speak to him, you can."

Hiram shook his head, and the old man continued the conversation on the phone, getting more irritable. "All right then, I don't know why, perhaps they're running short. He says I can have 'em. Now see you don't forget. Bring 'em. Anything else? Well, me clean things, me washing, oh yes, and bring me a Western, one I haven't read. I don't know how you know what I haven't read, just try, all right?" The phone at the other end went dead, and the old man handed the phone back to Hiram.

"She'll bring 'em. She always moans and groans about everything, I dunno why, considering I'm in here I'm not much trouble to her. Yes she'll bring 'em." He leaned back on the pillow and suddenly his eyes opened wide and he looked at Hiram suspiciously.

"I'm not going to take mine, you know, if I can get the hospital ones. Don't you forget that."

"No, I won't," said Hiram. He felt again that tiredness that always descended on him in the early morning. He unplugged the phone and wheeled it down the ward, and one or two of the old men said, "I'd like to use that," but Hiram shook his head and wheeled it by them.

"It's too early," he said and left them behind him, muttering and grumbling. He pushed the phone back down the corridor and parked it again by the lift. That meant tonight there would be some pills. He just hoped John never started asking for uppers. He seemed all right at the moment; he got them somewhere else. They were hard to get, but not impossible.

Usually John managed to buy them here and there, but sometimes he got sick of buying and said he expected Hiram to get them free . . .

Suddenly he felt an unbearable depression added to his tiredness.

Back in the children's ward, Carmichael felt she couldn't still the trembling in her limbs. She forced herself to sit down at the desk in the middle of the ward and finish writing the morning report. The night was nearly over. She could hear her junior nurse clattering in the kitchen; she hoped she wouldn't wake any of the babies. She went down to the nursery and looked at them. They were all quiet. One stirred as she walked in; two tiny fists came up from under the cot blanket. She automatically covered it, walked back into the ward, and sat down again.

She sat there for a long time, and depression settled over her like a black, black cloud. She felt she didn't care any more; if all the children in the ward died, she just wouldn't care. She'd blotted her copybook now for good, and to add to her worries she had heard that the nurse who was to relieve her on night duty was sick, so it might be that she would be on this hated ward longer if there was no one to replace her.

Carmichael finished writing the report, got up from the desk, and walked into the kitchen. "I may have to stay on here. Barton's off sick," she said to the nurse.

Her junior nodded. "So I heard, poor old you. Don't take too much notice of that old bitch," she said. "Sorry, me language again, dear. I know what you're going to say," and she turned her smiling, happy face round to Carmichael.

"How can you feel like that, when you've just been reprimanded and talked to like Hughes talked to you?" asked Car-michael.

"It doesn't worry me; besides, that was ages ago, old devil. After all, I can go and work somewhere else," said the nurse airily. "I could get married; me boy-friend wants to get mar-ried. He hasn't got enough to keep me, but at least I could get a job somewhere else. I don't rely on this bitchy lot. Don't want to either; it's because you care so much you get upset."

Carmichael knew that she was right, and yet how could she change her personality?

"Go and see to that child at the top of the ward. I can hear it."

"You've got sharp ears," said the nurse, smiling. She heard the call and then the sudden wail, "Nurse." She left the kitchen, and Carmichael stood at the sink, looking down at the now empty, greasy plates and the knives and forks. She picked up one knife and fingered it. It wasn't really sharp. She turned suddenly and opened the drawer in the kitchen table. There were two knives in there: a bread knife with a saw edge and a bigger, carving knife. She wondered idly what that was used for in this kitchen. She had seen it there before. They didn't carve meat up here; that wasn't the hospital way. They carved the meat when it was cold and put hot gravy on it to make it go farther: that was why it tasted like leather.

Carmichael took out the wooden-handled, long carving knife. She put it on the kitchen table and looked down at it. Her mind felt strange, confused. The light from the bare electric bulb above glittered on the knife. Without knowing she had picked it up, she found herself holding the knife in a striking position in her hand. She dropped it, trembling even more, and put her hands over her face just as her junior walked in. She saw her drop the knife and heard it clatter on the table.

"He's all right, the child I mean," she said. "What's the matter? What are you doing with that?"

Carmichael raised a white face and looked at her. "I don't know," she answered.

"What were you doing with that knife?" her junior asked curiously. She came over and picked up the carving knife, still looking at Carmichael.

"Put it back, put it back, put it back in the drawer," said Nurse Carmichael sharply, almost hysterically.

"All right, all right," said the nurse and dropped the knife noisily into the drawer and slammed it to.

"You'll wake the babies," said Nurse Carmichael automatically.

"They're waking anyway," said the nurse. Then suddenly she said, "Look, Staff, you don't think you should ask for a few nights off, do you? Say your grandmother's died or something. What you need is a bit of a change, you know. Go and stay with one of your relatives or have a bit of a knees-up. You do need it, really you do. You're as white as a sheet, and look at you, trembling all over. Sit down a minute."

"I haven't any relatives. Mind your own business, Nurse. I'm perfectly all right. Go back and get on with your work. If the children are waking, you can start fixing up some of them; that will give us more time." She suddenly sank down onto the kitchen chair. "Sorry, I didn't mean to snap at you."

"O.K. Just as you say," said the junior, but she went out of the kitchen, looking back at Nurse Carmichael, still with a look of half surprise and half worry in her eyes.

Morning. Marion Hughes had finished for the night. She felt rather more complacent than she had expected. The impact of Sir James's rebuff to her flirtatious advance had been deadened by his quick reaction to the name of Manton Hall. That would make him think, she thought.

The senior nursing officer had walked in and said, "Good morning, Miss Hughes, a quiet night?"

Marion had nodded and said, "Yes, I'm ready to give you the report."

The two women sat down at the desk, and Marion Hughes opened the big book which told the senior nursing officer and herself what had been going on in every part of the hospital during the night.

Who had been admitted, who had been operated on, who had been suddenly taken ill, who had had to go into Intensive Care. Just exactly what the Casualty programme had been. Whether any nurse had gone off sick during the night.

Marion Hughes reported efficiently. She did not forget the little oddments, like the dirty finger-marks on the Casualty door.

"Yes, I've noticed that," said the S.N.O. hastily. "The paint's due for washing. The nurses aren't supposed to clean the paint."

"I should have thought that just a damp cloth and a little scouring powder would have been all that was necessary to rub that off in about two minutes," said Marion Hughes dryly.

"Oh, that wouldn't do at all. Supposing a senior saw them. It's not included in the nurse's day, you know." The S.N.O. tried to make the scene a little lighter, something that was always difficult with Marion Hughes.

"I'm aware of that. I sometimes wonder what the nurse's day consists of," said Marion Hughes coldly. "They're not supposed to do this, they're not supposed to do that. One wonders exactly what they are supposed to do. However—" She dismissed it and got up. The S.N.O. rose too and threw down a newspaper on the top of the book. It fell open and revealed the whole of the front page. Marion Hughes looked at it abstractedly. "Any news, any more strikes?" she asked.

"Don't think so," said the S.N.O. "I've hardly had time to look yet."

Marion Hughes flicked over a page. Down in the corner was a small picture of a man. She looked idly at the caption. He'd been thrown from his horse while playing polo and badly injured. He rated a picture because he'd been in Prince Charles's team. She looked again at the photograph. Then suddenly it came back to her where she had seen Nigel Denton's face before. In a newspaper, but why, and in what newspaper? Her retentive and eager memory searched, like machinery set in motion, but she couldn't think. She remembered his face though. Where had it been? In the middle of the page? At the top of the page? No, she thought, on an inner page, down in the corner, like this one, that was all she could remember. Then the S.N.O. broke into her thoughts.

"Seen someone you know?" she asked.

"No, just someone who looks like someone I know," said Marion Hughes. She turned and said, "See you tonight," and went out and closed the door behind her, still thinking of that small photograph in the newspaper, with the caption underneath. It would come back to her; her memory never let her down. She was certain she would remember where she had seen that picture of Nigel Denton and remember why it had been there.

After a good deal of thought, accompanied by a good deal of anxiety, Sir James decided that he must arrange some kind of meeting with Marion Hughes, to find out just what she knew about Manton Hall: whether it was the child or whether it was anything else.

He thought carefully about where he would take her and decided on a road-house about fifteen miles away. He'd seen colleagues there at week-ends occasionally, but he was going to invite her for a week night; he would find out when her nights off were. He thought, he wasn't sure, that they had four at a time, something like that. He doubted that he would meet anyone he knew there, but if he did, well he would probably think that he was taking her out as a courtesy. Everyone in the hospital would know by now that she had assisted him with Lady Marshall's operation, but he hoped that not many people knew that he had been called in over Gordon Mayes's head, as it were. Anyway, it would cover, he hoped, anyone's speculation if he were seen, but he doubted, in midweek, that anyone would be there from the hospital at least.

He rang Marion Hughes's flat at ten o'clock in the morning, hoping that she would have arrived home. She answered it immediately.

"Oh, Sir James, how nice." The familiar voice with its upward lilt at the end was not surprised but sounded almost as if she had been waiting for the call.

"I wonder," Sir James's voice was stiff, "if you would care to dine with me one evening, when you have a night off? Out at Castlefield, you know the road-house there, the Clay Pigeon?"

"No," answered Marion Hughes coolly. "I don't know it, but I've heard a lot about it."

"They give one a very adequate meal," said Sir James and Marion Hughes smiled at the caution in his voice. She could tell that he felt slightly at a loss, undecided how to proceed with her.

"When are your—er—when are your nights off?"

"In two nights' time I have four nights off," she replied.

"What about Tuesday or Wednesday?" Sir James said quickly, too quickly, and Marion Hughes smiled again. The middle of the week was safer. She could tell that was what he was thinking, but she didn't particularly mind.

"That will be very nice," she said.

"Shall I call for you at the—at your flat?" Sir James paused, and she answered quickly.

"Yes, what time do you think we should leave, seven o'clock?" Again the upward inflection.

"Yes, that'll be all right." Sir James had hesitated a little before replying, and his voice was not as sharp as usual. He knew himself that he sounded unsettled and uncertain, and he felt that at the other end of the line Marion Hughes would be smiling to herself, feeling that she had already got him at a disadvantage.

"Well, you know where I live. I'll expect you about seven."

"No, I don't know where your flat is," Sir James said, determined not to let her think he had been looking up her address, but her reply took him off balance again.

"Oh, you knew my telephone number. I thought you would have looked it up in the book, Sir James, and therefore would have seen at the same time where I live."

Touché, he thought ruefully and said, "Yes, I've got your address, but I wasn't quite sure . . . oh yes, I do know the road, of course. I'll be there at seven, and we can talk about . . . Manton Hall Hospital. I'm sure we're going to find out that we have many mutual acquaintances."

"I'm sure we shall," said Marion Hughes.

The night before Marion Hughes started her nights off, the round went almost without criticism.

She had been for once benign and pleasant. Nurse Carmichael came in for some slight sarcasm when Miss Hughes went into the kitchen, as she put it, smiling, "to see if anything is cooking—isn't that what they say, Nurse?" Nurse Carmichael had not answered and tried to ignore the remark.

The ward rounds finished, Marion Hughes had come down to Casualty and found to her surprise Nigel Denton with a patient, as well as Dr. Creasey.

"What's happening, Nurse?" she said genially to the Casualty staff nurse. Her attitude to this girl since the Lady Marshall affair had softened considerably, and the girl simpered.

"A query abdomen of some sort, Miss Hughes. I don't quite know what."

"Query abdomen? Why wasn't her own doctor called to her then? Why was she brought into Casualty?" asked Miss Hughes somewhat sharply.

"I think she works in a night-club. They brought her straight here by ambulance. She doesn't seem very bad, but she's in quite a lot of pain. That's why Miss Creasey got Mr. Denton to look at her."

"I see." Marion Hughes went through into the Casualty area, and over to the couch, pulling back the corner of the curtain as she entered the cubicle.

"An admission, doctor?" She looked first at Dr. Creasey, and as she didn't answer she looked at Nigel Denton, who was gently palpating the girl's white abdomen.

Miss Hughes looked at the patient's face. She was undeniably pretty, but over made-up, with heavy blue eye-shadow and a sprinkling of scintillating dust over that, accentuated by thick false eyelashes that seemed almost to weigh the eyelids down. Her mouth was scarlet with lipstick, while rouge high on each cheekbone brought out the pallor of the rest of her face. Marion Hughes noticed too that across her upper lip and on her forehead were tiny beads of perspiration. She automati-

cally reached past Dr. Creasey and took the girl's pulse. It was
120 or more. Marion Hughes judged that without looking at
her watch and then withdrew her hand.

"Yes, I'm afraid we'll have to take you in, young lady," said
Nigel Denton. The big eyes fought with the lashes as she
raised them with difficulty and looked at him.

"Oh Lord, that means I may lose my job. What's the matter with me?" she asked anxiously.

"Nothing very terrible. I think perhaps you've got an inflamed appendix, but rather a nasty one," he said.

"I've had it before, what they call a grumbling appendix,"
said the girl, and she suddenly bit her lower lip, showing more
anxiety.

"It's nothing," said Nigel Denton reassuringly. "It's quite a
run of the mill operation. You'll soon be home."

"It's not that," said the girl. "It will make a scar, won't it?
It will make a scar down there." She pointed to the area
where she had most pain, just below the navel on the right-
hand side.

"I'm a stripper, you see," she said. "I can't afford to have a
scar. Will it be a big one?"

"Just a little one," said Nigel. He paused before he said it,
and a strange expression came over his face; and in that pause
Marion remembered where she had seen Nigel Denton's face
before, remembered the caption under the picture:

YOUNG DOCTOR ACCIDENTALLY KILLS WIFE

Nigel Denton looked up at her and in that second realized
that she had remembered where she had seen his face before.
She must have read about him. He felt a surge of the old
panic and guilt. Marion Hughes spoke softly, not taking her
eyes from Denton's face.

"Don't worry. I'm sure Mr. Denton will make the scar as
small as possible. He knows about these things, you see, and

after all"—she dropped her eyes and met those of the patient
—"it's not as if you'd been in a car accident, is it?" She
looked up again at Nigel Denton and their eyes met and held,
and as she leaned forward she caught the smell of whisky on
his breath. She turned abruptly on her heel and walked out of
Casualty.

"What was all that about?" asked Dr. Creasey, half smiling
at Denton's expression.

"Nothing," he answered almost harshly. "Nothing at the
moment, anyway." Then he turned back to the girl on the
couch and said, "Well, young lady, we'd better see what we
can do for you now, eh?"

During Marion Hughes's nights off, several things happened
to keep her memory fresh in everyone's mind and to dispel to
some extent the feeling of security her absence always
brought.

Nurse Carmichael was sent for at eight thirty in the morning by the senior nursing officer and reprimanded sternly: first
for the mistake in the child's temperature, found an hour after
she had taken it; then for cooking in the kitchen, when she
was reminded that eating hospital food was tantamount to
stealing; and finally for asking a junior to break a rule, which
showed a complete lack of responsibility.

Carmichael had merely stood in front of the senior nursing
officer's desk and said nothing. There had been a long pause
and then the S.N.O. had asked, "Surely there is enough food
supplied in the canteen to stop one needing to eat in the
hospital ward kitchen?"

All Carmichael had been able to do was to nod miserably.
It was one of the most humiliating experiences she had suf-

fered since she had begun her training and qualified as a staff nurse. She felt she was being talked to as if she were the merest junior, all chances of promotion disappearing as she watched the S.N.O.'s stern face. She walked out of the office after the senior nurse had said, "You may go now. Please don't let this kind of thing happen again."

When Carmichael had left the office, she had felt that even applying for the post of surgical ward sister was a waste of time. That day had been terrible. She hadn't slept at all. She spent most of the day walking round the local park seeing nothing; children running round her, dogs running round her, elderly ladies sitting down in the early morning sunshine, it had all been remote from her, nothing to her. Her thoughts went round and round. Shall I leave this hospital and apply for a post somewhere else? But then what's my reference going to be like? Shall I give up nursing altogether? Her depression was so great that she felt disoriented. At the end of the afternoon she went back to her bed-sitter and lay on the bed just gazing and gazing at the ceiling, wondering what the hell to do, and dreading the time when she had to go back on duty that night.

The only grain of comfort was that Marion Hughes would be on nights off. She hoped too that her junior nurse wouldn't have heard, or wouldn't hear, about "Poor old Carmichael being torn up by the S.N.O." She cringed at the thought of talk of that kind. Her seniority was so precious to her. It was all Miss Hughes's fault; every bit of it was Miss Hughes. An ordinary, decent night super would have understood that a child could fling a temperature like that in half an hour, though she did admit to herself that she had never known a child to do it before. Then the cooking thing; another night super might have said, "What do you think you're doing, you two, having a nosh up in the middle of the night? You'd better do something about this. I won't notice it this time."

That's what the junior night super would have said; but perhaps that's why she is still junior, thought Carmichael. Not Miss Hughes; every tiny single thing must be reported. She was looking to show her efficiency; she was looking for promotion. From night superintendent, she would get an S.N.O.'s post, and then go still farther up and become chief nursing officer.

Miss Hughes would get up on other people's backs, thought Carmichael dismally, on other people's backs; I could kill her, she thought. She's climbing up on mine as well as everybody else's.

The hatred that filled her almost frightened her. She thought of herself in the children's ward kitchen a couple of nights ago and turned her head on one side. Tears rolled out of her eyes and down to the pillow. She knew she'd go on duty that night with one of her ghastly tension headaches. She thought: it's just too much, all of it.

Hiram Jones was feeling the glorious relief of just having Miss Norman, the junior night superintendent, coming round. She was relaxed and jolly, and rounds were a joy. He thought, again and again, if only this could go on. If bloody Miss Hughes would leave, this job would be tenable.

John was getting more difficult; that didn't help. But he would probably get a few more Nembutals while Miss Hughes was away, because although old Mr. Butterworth had told him that his daughter hadn't brought in his Nembutals as she'd promised on the phone, he did not believe him. That night he was determined to give the old man his sleeping pills, not hold them back for John in the morning.

He'd have to take them off another patient or John would

have to do without; he wanted Mr. Butterworth to sleep soundly, he might even give him three Nembutals as a treat. Then Hiram wanted to go through the old man's locker during his junior's rest hour. If he couldn't get some for John soon, he was afraid John would leave him, and that would finish him completely.

With this job, John made everything possible. To go home to him, to know you had somebody loving waiting for you. Even the fact that that petulant lower lip often stuck out made him more precious to Hiram in some ways, more lovable, more sexy perhaps. Sometimes Hiram wished he didn't love the boy so much and wondered, if he didn't produce any pills ever again, whether John would stay with him. Sometimes he doubted it. He prayed it wasn't just the pills, just drugs. He hoped to God it wasn't.

When he did the round to give out the sleeping pills, the last medicine to those who needed them, he came last to Mr. Butterworth. "Are you sure you've not got that bottle? Are you sure your daughter didn't bring it in?"

"Yes, I am," said the old man. "I jolly well am, and I want some. I know I can have them; I asked the doctor this morning."

"I know, I know, I only asked," said Hiram. He took three capsules of Nembutal from the medicine trolley and brought them to Mr. Butterworth with a glass of water.

"There you are," he said. "You can have three tonight and be sure of getting a good night."

"Three!" The old man chuckled gleefully. No wonder they'd stopped giving them Nembutal, thought Hiram. It was addictive all right, and the sooner the last patients were off it the better, but they were afraid of withdrawal symptoms, particularly with these old men.

"Three," said the old man again. "Oh, good. What's the matter with you?" He looked up at Hiram Jones, cramming the capsules in his mouth and golloping down the water, almost as if he were afraid that Hiram would change his mind.

"Oh, nothing," said Hiram Jones. "Just got a few more tonight, Miss Hughes being off."

"Yes, *that* bitch," said Mr. Butterworth. "Nice when she's off, isn't it? Nicer in the morning as well. Norman doesn't take any notice of well, anything much, does she? I like her."

Hiram nodded. He wasn't going to talk about a nurse to a patient. He padded off down the ward, wheeling the medicine trolley squeakily in front of him. He'd only got to wait until Butterworth dropped off into a sound sleep, and he'd have everything out of that locker and find that bottle of Nembutal, if it was there, and he was pretty sure it was.

Everything was relaxed. When he came back from the medicine round, he found his junior in the kitchen, pouring a bottle of the old men's beer. "Want one? May as well make hay while the cat's away."

"Make hay while the cat's away. What the devil do you mean by that?" said Hiram.

"Mixing me metaphors, you know," said the junior. Hiram nodded in agreement to the glass of beer and Atkins poured one out and gave it to him.

"Dear old Carmichael on the kids' ward got it good and proper," said the junior male nurse, looking at Hiram with a grin. "Not much of a looker, is she? A wreck, if you ask me. Looks as if she's going through a nervous breakdown. Her junior says she's absolute hell to work for, because she's so worried about old Hughesie. Well, she's got old Hughesie's nights off to revel in now. Hope she makes the most of it and gets all the eggs and chips, illicit sleeps, and a bit of sex even, although with her looks I doubt it."

Hiram Jones had drunk the beer with appreciation, but as he finished it and put the glass on the table, he said, "Oh, shut up. All you think about is hospital scandal."

"Well, there's plenty of that in a small way," said his junior with a wink. "And after all, it helps to pass the nights away. How's John?" he finished up.

Hiram Jones ignored him and went back into the ward.

On the Tuesday evening that Sir James and Marion Hughes had arranged to have dinner together, he arrived promptly at seven. She heard the Rover draw up outside and looked out of her window. In a way she was gratified. He could have tried to put her in her place, by keeping her waiting, in an effort to show that he wasn't the least nervous of what she knew about him and Manton Hall Hospital.

She waited, heard the car door slam, then, a moment or two later, the ring at her flat door. She delayed opening it for a few moments, went through to her bedroom, sprayed a little more of her perfume from the atomiser onto her neck, and came out and opened the door to him. "Good evening, Sir James. How pleasant to see you. Do come in," she said.

He hesitated on the doorstep, rather, she thought to her amusement, like a fly not wanting to enter the spider's web, but after a second or two's hesitation he entered and said, "Good evening to you, Miss Hughes. I've booked a table for half-past seven, so we had better . . ."

Marion Hughes conceded graciously. "Of course. I was going to offer you a drink, but if you'd rather go straightaway I'm quite ready." She went back into the bedroom to fetch her coat, then held it out to him. He took it from her and slipped it expertly round her shoulders. She was wearing a blue dress she had bought that day, especially for the occasion. She was pleased with it. It was exactly right, and she hoped that Sir James would consider she was dressed in good taste. Whatever he felt did not show in his expression. He turned and preceded her downstairs and out to the car.

The drive to the road-house was conducted almost in complete silence. There was a strange tenseness between them, and Marion Hughes found it difficult to talk naturally. Her few tentative remarks were greeted with monosyllabic replies, so after a few miles she ceased to talk and sat there quietly planning how the conversation would go when they were actually seated together at the same table.

On the whole the dinner went well. Marion reminisced lightly about Manton Hall Hospital. "Do you remember Dr. Julian White, Sir James?" she asked during the first course, and Sir James nodded, rather absently, though his face showed some expression.

"Indeed I do," he said. "He was the consultant who dressed so peculiarly and wore no socks. Am I right?" His voice was light but still guarded.

"That's right. We were naughty. We used to laugh at him behind his back. He was a great figure of fun but a very good physician, did you not think so?"

"Yes, I did, a very good physician," said Sir James.

The second course arrived and Marion Hughes felt that the mention of the senior physician at Manton Hall Hospital would lead nicely into the subject she wished to bring forward. "Of course, you would remember him well, Sir James. There was that child, wasn't there, and he spoke up for you very well."

"That child?" Sir James looked at her.

"Yes, Julian Longford, you remember. The little boy who was given an overdose of intrathecal penicillin. It had a tremendous effect on the hospital, didn't it, and I'm sure on you. The child's parents—he was an only child. I remember him being brought in—I'd never seen a case of meningitis before. Those terrible cries, and the head bent back. I was so stupid then, so young. I thought as they put him in the bed that he was looking at the cherry trees outside the window, but of course . . ."

"I doubt if he could have seen the cherry trees," said Sir James dryly, and Marion Hughes felt she wasn't getting quite the right reaction. She had expected more surprise, more dismay, at the fact that she knew of this incident. She enlarged on it a little.

"Of course, you were exonerated, weren't you? That's what I meant about Dr. White—he was so helpful."

"There was no need for him to be helpful," said Sir James, again in that dry, almost toneless voice. "I was exonerated because of the facts; the bottle handed to me was an overdose and I used it. Unhappily, the nurse didn't show me the bottle before I drew up the penicillin."

"No, that was of course wrong of her," said Marion Hughes. "But then, the ultimate responsibility, as they say, is always with the doctor, don't they?"

"Yes." Sir James continued his meal.

Marion Hughes was puzzled. Why was he so unmoved? She'd expected a much greater reaction from him than this. "Well, it's in the past now, and nobody I expect knows about it, or do they?" The upward inflection sounded almost menacing, and Sir James noted it and smiled inwardly. If this was all the ammunition she had against him, for whatever it was she wanted to force him to do, it wasn't much. But had she more ammunition? Did she know about the girl and the abortion? That he had to know.

They were having their coffee and a brandy. Sir James was looking remarkably relaxed. Marion Hughes felt a tension in herself; things were not going her way. What was happening? Didn't he mind? Had she overestimated his wish to conceal the facts, the facts about the child? Perhaps they already knew at St. Jude's? No, she didn't think so. Perhaps she was underestimating his reaction. Perhaps he was taking it less calmly underneath. He was a man used to hiding his feelings.

"More coffee or another brandy, Miss Hughes?" Sir James asked, and Marion Hughes answered,

"Perhaps a little more coffee, Sir James. It is delicious."

"Yes, they make very good coffee," said Sir James and summoned the waiter. He was the kind of man, thought Marion, who when he summoned the waiter, the waiter came. That was nice. Then he turned the conversation.

"When you were a cadet at Manton Hall, did you know many of the nurses?" he asked.

"Well, no," Marion Hughes hesitated. "As cadets, of course, we lived out. I lived at home actually. We weren't encouraged to have much to do with the nurses already in training; perhaps they thought it might put us off." She smiled. "We met them on the ward, of course, and in the dining room."

"Did you meet a young nurse called Theresa O'Sullivan?" He had to know. He tried to keep the tension out of his voice and make the question sound of mild interest, as if he were asking about the daughter of an old friend, or a fellow consultant, but Marion Hughes was not deceived.

She met his eyes across the table and noticed the pulse in his temple was beating rapidly. Why? . . . No, she had never met, or couldn't remember meeting, a young nurse called Theresa O'Sullivan, but something warned her not to tell Sir James that. So she said casually, "Oh, Theresa O'Sullivan, the little Irish girl. Yes, I knew her."

Sir James signalled to the waiter. "Another brandy, please. Are you sure . . . ?" Marion Hughes shook her head.

When the brandy arrived, Sir James drank it quickly and then stood up. "Shall we go?" he said, and as abruptly she nodded.

While he was putting the coat round her shoulders, ever

polite, prior to bringing her home, she turned to him and said, "Sir James, we all felt so sorry about your wife. I do hope your little holiday, and break from duty, has helped you to get over the shock."

His face didn't soften in the least. He nodded, and his completely noncommittal attitude stung her into going on. "It was such a pity, too, that she didn't come into hospital three months before; apparently they might have been able to do more for her. That often happens, doesn't it, with doctors' wives. They're ill, but often their illness is ignored. They are the last to get treatment."

He looked at her with absolute hatred. She felt perhaps she had made a mistake, pushed things too far.

"I don't know what you mean by that remark, Miss Hughes," he said. "And I can't think how you have come to that conclusion. Most certainly had I known she was as ill as she was, I would have made her come into hospital earlier. Unfortunately, she was not a woman to complain."

The drive home was made in complete silence. When they arrived at her flat, he got out and came round and opened the door for her, then, with cold courtesy, accompanied her up the steps to her flat door. She got the key out of her evening bag and said, "Thank you, thank you for a most pleasant evening, Sir James."

He made no answer, but with a brief "Good night, Miss Hughes" ran down the steps, got into his car, and drove rapidly away.

Back in her flat Marion Hughes was not quite sure that she had handled the situation as well as she might. She would try to get him to take her out again, that she must do, and the next time she could afford to be charming, very charming. She feared a rebuff, but surely he knew now where he stood. He wasn't a fool. He knew that if he ignored her from now on, she could tell about the child, she could even suggest that perhaps Lady Hatfield . . . She hadn't heard that through the hospital grape-vine. She had been passing the theatre changing room and had heard Gordon Mayes say, "If only we'd seen her three months ago she might not have been inoperable." She had stored the remark up for possible future use. By Sir James's reaction, it might well have been the truth.

There was no question in her mind that Sir James had ignored his wife's illness, not with any particular evil intent. No, it was just a question of priorities, but she felt that he had a feeling of guilt about it. It was just how doctors sometimes were, too busy to notice any symptoms in their own family, so poor Lady Hatfield . . . Her mind went back over the conversation. The child had not made the impact that she had expected. Then she remembered . . . Why had he asked about that Irish girl? What was her name? . . . Theresa something. That was strange. Marion Hughes slipped out of her dress and hung it up in the wardrobe, went over and sat down in front of the dressing-table, opened a jar of cream, to clean the make-up off her face, and put it down . . . tapped her forefinger nail against her teeth reflectively while looking at herself in the mirror. Theresa O'Sullivan, that was the name.

When Sir James got home he felt more tired than if he'd just done a long operating list. The whole incident of Julian Longford had been brought back to him by that bitch. As she had spoken, he had remembered the cherry trees and that fat, pleasant, ward sister, who had pointed them out to him so often, as they waved their branches of pink flowers against the blue sky in the spring, during their short life.

Short life. He thought again of Julian, that child, five years old. He remembered every single movement during that lumbar puncture. He remembered the mother's and the father's faces as they stood there listening to the news of their child's death. After so much optimism had been shown them by the medical and nursing staff, now their child was dead. He'd been the one to tell them. It had made him remember his own tiredness twenty years ago; so much work was expected, and there were so few people to do it. Not like today where a house surgeon's half-day was as sacrosanct as Holy Writ, and there were more doctors to relieve the pressure. He poured himself out a large brandy and tried to reconstruct the conversation. Would it matter if it came out about the child? It would be a nine days' wonder, a storm in a teacup; hospitals were famous for those, but he would rather it didn't happen. He knew himself to be almost too severe about the faults of his juniors. This story being repeated round the hospital wouldn't help. Then there was that last remark about his wife. It had been true, but how the hell did she know? Lottie hadn't complained, not enough for him to make her do something about it, get it investigated. The worst thing of all was her knowing that girl, that child Theresa. He could remember her vividly. Their brief affair, so stupid. She was a virgin, too, and a Roman Catholic. The whole thing had been traumatic, disgusting, and then the aftermath. If anyone had found out that, found it out now . . . Just how much did she know? Young girls chattered together, especially at that age, and especially in that situation. Theresa was a talkative little thing and tearful and almost hysterical when she had found out she was pregnant. He felt she would have told anyone, anyone sympathetic enough to listen.

Yes, the obviously new dress, the careful make-up, the flirtatious looks, everything pointed to the fact that she was after
him. Well, he'd see her in hell before he married her.

There was Madeleine. Good God, to compare the two! No,
Marion Hughes would have to be silenced somehow. He'd
have to . . . He suddenly felt too tired to go on thinking. He
poured another brandy and sat down again feeling gloomy and
threatened.

Marion Hughes's nights off went by and she returned to the
hospital; and on her return the tension on night duty
mounted in every ward and department.

Hiram Jones, in spite of the precious three capsules given to
Mr. Butterworth on the first night, had not managed to find
the bottle of Nembutal. He felt sure the old man was secret-
ing it somewhere. He'd searched his locker thoroughly to no
avail; the old man must be stuffing the bottle under his mat-
tress, or under his pillow, and he daren't look there for fear of
waking him. Tonight he stood looking down at the sleeping
Mr. Butterworth speculatively. Should he go through the
whole ritual again and have everything out of the locker, while
his junior, Atkins, was at rest hour, or should he give the
whole thing up for lost? Perhaps the old man was not lying
after all and hadn't got the bottle, but somehow . . .

The old man stirred in his sleep and Hiram drew back a
little. As he did so, he noticed on the locker top a box of
tissues, a large box labelled TISSUES FOR MEN. It was half
empty and Hiram noticed that one end bulged slightly. He
whistled softly to himself and put his hand in the space left by
the missing tissues. There was the Nembutal. He drew out the
tan-coloured plastic bottle, with the black screw top, and read

with difficulty in the light of the night-light: *R. Whittaker—Dispensing Chemist—Mr. Butterworth;* and under that, written in ink: *Nembutal. Take one at night, as directed.* Hiram turned the bottle over, and the capsules fell about with a dry rattle. There were at least forty-five, maybe more. Hiram slipped them into the pocket of his uniform with a sigh of relief. He looked at Mr. Butterworth, still snoring away happily, and walked softly out of the ward and into the kitchen.

"Thank God, I've got them," he said softly to himself. He unscrewed the cap and poured the capsules onto the table, putting them back two by two into the bottle, and as he did so he counted: 36, 38..........50, 52, 54, 56. That wasn't bad. The G.P. must have prescribed sixty, and old Butterworth had only been given four, two for two nights probably, by his daughter. It was a marvellous bonus, something that Hiram badly needed with John in his present mood.

He got up, went into the ward, and came back into the kitchen carrying a manilla envelope. He tipped the pills out of the bottle again: 2, 4, 6, 8..........20. He put them into the envelope. That would do to be going on with. He sealed the envelope, dropped it into his overall pocket, and screwed the cap back onto the plastic bottle. He was about to go back to the ward and replace it by Mr. Butterworth's bed when his junior nurse walked into the kitchen. Hiram hastily dropped the bottle into his overall pocket with the envelope.

"Back already? Your time's not up yet, is it?" he said in surprise.

"No, I haven't had me time off. I've been sent back. Big excitement," said his junior. "You're to go down to Casualty. There's a crash of some kind coming in, don't know what, but a bus full I think, forty or so; that's what the ambulance people say. They'll be here in half an hour. Don't know any more details. I expect there'll be three people with cut fingers in the end—they always exaggerate—but that's the message."

Hiram felt a surge of excitement: to get away from Stenton ward, just for a bit, would be lovely. The excitement of Casualty was something he'd missed. He'd done quite a stint of Casualty during training. He'd liked it.

"Well, everything's been pretty quiet while you've been away," he said. "Don't think I've had a single buzz, so probably you'll get it all now."

Atkins nodded gloomily.

"Old Machin even. He's only asked for a couple of bottles and then gone off to sleep again."

"Maybe they all had their pills last night, eh?" Atkins looked at Hiram, with his head cocked on one side.

Hiram chose to ignore the remark. "You can get on with the report," he said. "Goodness knows when I'll be back. If it's a real major disaster I'll be there till the day staff come on, so see you get everything right for old Hughesie, if she manages a round, won't you?"

"Don't worry, I will. Have a nice time and don't faint at the sight of blood," said his junior.

Hiram came out of the kitchen and looked into the ward. All was quiet. He made his way along the corridor and down the stairs towards Casualty.

In the Casualty department all the lights were on; it was obvious that each nurse knew what she was to do, and all the correct people had been called in. The business of a major disaster had been talked over, a committee set up, procedure settled on, and was now being called into motion.

Two porters, normally on day duty, but who had been called in the moment the accident was reported, were bringing in mattresses and arranging them on the floor along one wall of the Casualty waiting-room, and a pile of more mattresses was being put outside. These would be used for the badly injured, because the Casualty department had only six couches, which might well not be enough. According to a nurse Hiram asked, a bus with about thirty-five men in it had crashed. They had all been to a party given by their firm. An orderly holding a large armful of plastic aprons was stationed at the door of the waiting-room to greet each doctor, nurse, or porter. She handed one to Hiram as he walked in and motioned with her head towards the changing room to indicate that he was to go through, take off his white coat, put on the plastic apron, and join the throng waiting for the casualties to arrive.

Marion Hughes was there, cool and efficient as usual. She was talking to a plastic-aproned Nigel Denton as Hiram walked in. He went up and reported to her. She gave him a cool nod, and he went on into the Casualty area.

He could see in the Clinic room a nurse laying up trolleys for injections: anti-tetanus, morphine, anti-gangrene. She could give at once anything the doctor ordered and would mark the patient's forehead accordingly with an indelible pencil. It was a foolproof system and meant that no patient would receive the same injection twice.

Dr. Creasey joined Mr. Denton and Miss Hughes, and Hiram heard Miss Hughes say in her crisp voice, "Sir James has been notified and Mr. Mayes."

"And the Orthopod?" broke in Denton.

"Of course," Miss Hughes said coldly. "Everyone who should be notified has been notified, Mr. Denton."

Dr. Creasey and Nigel exchanged glances, and the casualty officer looked heavenwards as Miss Hughes turned away to greet Sir James, who, followed by Gordon Mayes, had just walked in.

"I must say she's got everything going quickly," said Miss

Creasey to Denton, looking down with amusement at her plastic apron. "At least we're all dressed for the job, even if nothing comes in."

"Anything in yet?" Sir James asked, taking off his coat.

Marion Hughes shook her head, at the same time signalling to a nurse to relieve Sir James of his coat.

"Take that and Mr. Mayes's through to the changing room and put them on hangers," she said, and at that moment they heard the wail of the siren of the first ambulance as it drew up at the Casualty entrance. A nurse went forward and propped open the plastic doors, and the first patient was wheeled in, his face pale above the red blanket which covered him. The ambulance man at the head of the trolley was holding the man's head to one side, over a vomit bowl, and he was being copiously sick. The smell of beer permeated the Casualty entrance. Denton motioned to the ambulance man to take the patient through to the Casualty area, and a porter came forward and guided the end of the trolley. They wheeled the man through, followed by Nigel.

At that moment Nurse Carmichael walked in, followed closely by another stretcher. She went hastily up to Miss Hughes and said, "It's my rest time, Miss Hughes. I'd like to help here, if I may." Marion Hughes hardly appeared to notice her, just nodded, and Carmichael scuttled through with her plastic apron into the changing area. When she came out, another stretcher was being wheeled in containing a man sitting upright, supporting himself on his arms, and declaiming loudly that he was all right, there was nothing the matter with him; he just wanted to get off the trolley and go to the lavatory.

Hiram's junior nurse had been right in his assumption that forty was a slight exaggeration, but there were thirty-two and that was quite enough for this Casualty department. More ambulances arrived with patients. Soon those with slight inju-

ries were sitting on a row of chairs in the waiting-room, while
those with major injuries were lying on the couches and mattresses being attended to by the general surgeons and the
casualty officer and the registrar. Even the house physician
was there.

Nigel looked round appreciatively. Everything was going
very smoothly. The phone was in constant use informing June
Fyldes up in the theatre what was coming up for the
orthopaedic surgeon, who was waiting there to deal with frac-
tures or any other bone injuries. Sir James and Gordon Mayes
were busy palpating abdomens, looking for internal injuries
and bleeding. George Hayward armed with an ophthalmo-
scope was peering into eyes, looking for unequal pupils which
might denote head injuries.

The police hovered about, at first interviewing the driver.
He had skidded, he said, quite suddenly. He was given a
breathalyser test, which was negative, found to be unhurt, and
told to wait outside in the Casualty waiting hall, away from
the injured. He looked white and shaken.

Hiram enjoyed the situation in which he found himself.
With his rolled-up sleeves and his plastic apron to protect him
from the blood, he walked about dealing with one patient
after another, feeling more of a nurse than he had done for
ages.

"Injection of tetanus, there, Nurse, please. I think this chap
will have to have an anti-gas gangrene, a nasty compound
fracture. Straight up to the ward." A nurse followed behind
Nigel Denton, filling in cards with names and addresses, asking the patients when they had last eaten. Unfortunately it
was mostly when they had last drunk; it had been a good party
given by the firm. It meant they couldn't be operated on for
at least four hours; if they needed an urgent operation, their
stomachs would have to be emptied by pump.

Marion Hughes could not be faulted, Denton had to admit.

He watched her, apron over her dress, sleeves rolled back, walking from one patient to another, taking pulses, blood pressures, entering them on the patient's card. She was like an efficient machine, he thought, and just about as human. But she undoubtedly was a good nurse, and if it were not for her unfortunate personality, she would be an asset to any hospital. As it was . . . As if she had read his thoughts, she turned round during a slight pause in her activities and wrinkled her nose.

"This smell of drink is quite disgusting, isn't it Mr. Denton?" No patient could hear her; she was careful of that.

Denton's eyes met hers, and he started to reply. "Yes, it's not very pleasant, particularly when it's been—"

But before he could finish, she continued. "I'm always very conscious of the smell of alcohol."

Nigel said nothing. Had she smelled his breath? He presumed she had, or she wouldn't have made this remark so pointedly. When? He tried to think. That night when the girl, the stripper, had come in with the appendicitis? He'd had one before that, but he'd done the operation faultlessly. She was dangerous, this woman. If she could report Creasey for sending a man home with hysterical chest pain, she could certainly report him for smelling of drink before going into the operating-theatre.

"It's difficult to tell, Miss Hughes," he said coldly, "whether a person has had half a pint of beer or eight pints, or one whisky or eighteen, just by the smell of his breath."

"There is a time and place for everything, Mr. Denton," she replied coldly. "I don't like the smell in Casualty tonight, but at least it's excusable. They have been to a party and not at work."

Did she mean anything? Nigel was almost certain she did, that she was getting at him in some way, but for the moment he thrust it out of his mind.

Denton walked into the Casualty theatre. A nurse had first helped a patient onto the table. He had a long gash in his arm from the glass of the bus window. It would mean about sixteen stitches, but there was no tendon injury and Denton felt he could leave it to the house physician. Then he saw he was engaged and decided to do the suturing himself.

He looked up at the nurse standing at the trolley on the other side of the Casualty operating table. It was Nurse Carmichael from the children's ward. He had met her once or twice on the rounds and remembered her vaguely: a scared, miserable-looking woman. Tonight the cheeks above her mask were flushed, but the eyes that met his were as worried as ever. She handed him the forceps with the needle clamped in the end. Denton looked at her.

"Local first, don't you think?" he said pleasantly.

Carmichael hastily put the forceps back on the trolley and picked up the loaded syringe.

"Sorry," she said, and Denton smiled and started to inject the long incision with local anaesthetic. The man on the table winced and Nigel turned to him and repeated the word Carmichael had said.

"Sorry, old chap. Once it's numb it will be easier for you. The sutures won't hurt. You're lucky it's such a nice, clean cut. It'll soon heal."

"It was bloody awful," the patient said. "Bloody awful. One minute we were all singing, you know, and the next we were over on our side, people fighting to get out, horrible. I shan't forget it in a hurry."

"You will," said Nigel Denton, gently putting the needle into the sides of the wound and injecting the anaesthetic.

"How are the others?" asked the man. "How many were badly injured, I mean? I saw old Tom Scorer. He'd only cut his finger, I think."

"Yes, probably he had. I don't know," answered Nigel Denton.

He didn't tell the man he'd just examined a Mr. Scorer, and his internal injuries had made him an immediate candidate for the theatre. They would all know about each other soon enough, and meanwhile the work, the patching up, the sewing up, the making well again, had to go on. By the look of it there were going to be no fatalities directly, anyway. Some were badly injured, but . . . That was something to be thankful for, that nobody had been brought in dead.

He looked up at Nurse Carmichael. She handed him the suturing forceps and her anxious eyes met his.

"Good work, Nurse," he said. He could tell, in spite of her mask, by the slight crinkling of her eyes, and the even more heightened flush on her cheeks, that she was smiling and that she was pleased to receive what he felt was a rare word of encouragement.

Hiram Jones really felt in his element, and as the Casualty department gradually cleared, and the ambulance took home those with only minor injuries, and others were wheeled up to the wards, he felt a sense of regret.

It had been so different. Time had flown. He looked at his watch: ten past seven, soon be time to go off duty. Of course there was the clearing up to do, and the day staff would be on soon; they wouldn't like to come on to a Casualty department that was a complete shambles. No, everything must be cleaned up ready for the day casualties and the normal dressing visits. It had been just an incident, and yet Hiram felt that if he got the chance he'd apply for another post, preferably in Casualty or an Out Patient department, where people were coming and going all the time. Perhaps if he were in a scene like this he wouldn't rely so much on John's company. He went on cleaning rubber pads, swilling down sinks, cleaning the theatre table, assisted by Carmichael and nurses drawn from other wards. They were all tired now. It had been an exciting time, and the reaction was setting in.

"Well, that's over," said Miss Hughes as she pulled down the cuffs of her dress and did the buttons up neatly as usual. She had been through to the changing room and taken off her plastic apron, and, by the look of it, touched up her make-up.

Nigel Denton looked at her. She looked exactly the same. Nothing could ruffle that woman, he thought. She didn't register tiredness or excitement or anything. He wondered what it would be like if she had crashed her car and had been brought into Casualty. Probably she would have looked just as neat and just as efficient and would tell the staff exactly what she wanted done. Nigel suddenly realized that he hated her. If she ever does crash her car, he thought, I hope she won't be brought into Casualty but into the damn morgue. He reproached himself. That was a terrible thing to think, even about this bloody woman.

"Good night, Mr. Denton. Thank you," Marion Hughes said.

Nigel said, "Good night, Miss Hughes. I hope the smell of drink doesn't haunt you too much."

She made no reply and turned on her heel, and at that moment saw Nurse Carmichael. "Nurse Carmichael," she said sharply. "You said you were coming into Casualty just for your rest hour. What are you still doing here? Have you left your ward in charge of the junior since 3 A.M.?"

"I told her to call me, if she needed me, Miss Hughes. I told her to phone me here, at once," stammered Carmichael.

"Really—then let me tell you that you have completely overstepped your authority this time, Nurse. Go back to your ward at once. We will talk about this when you come on duty tonight. I just hope no child has suffered in your absence. Go back at once."

Nurse Carmichael's face, pink with her efforts in the theatre and the unusual excitement, turned a pasty white and crinkled as if she were about to cry.

"I didn't think. I was so . . ." Her voice tapered off. She looked at Miss Hughes, her eyes pleading. Then, as Marion Hughes turned away, she rushed from the Casualty area and into the changing room. There the tears started pouring down her cheeks. This was too much; she just couldn't stand any more. She crushed herself up against the row of coats and pressed one to her face.

Hiram had heard Nigel Denton's remark to Miss Hughes about the smell of alcohol. "What was all that about, Mr. Denton?" he asked. "Didn't she like the smell of beer, then? I must admit it was pretty rough at the beginning, when they were being sick I mean."

"Something like that," said Denton.

Hiram gave a final wash to his hands, took off his plastic apron, looked it over critically to see if there was any blood on it that he hadn't cleaned off properly, then moved through to the changing room to hang it up with the rest. He walked through the Casualty area, into the waiting-room, calling good night to the nurses as he went into the changing room, where his overall was hanging, just as he'd left it. He hung up the apron, took down his white coat, and slipped it on. It had been a good night, he thought, a really exciting, different kind of night, and he would go home tired, but with a different kind of tiredness, and with the pilly willies. He thrust his hand in his pocket for the reassuring touch of the plastic bottle, but only the manilla envelope was there. The bottle had gone.

Marion Hughes returned to her office from Casualty well satisfied. It was the first major disaster they'd had since the new organization, the procedure part of which she'd been responsible for herself.

Her head ached slightly; from the tension and the heat in Casualty she supposed. She went up to her office mirror, repaired her face, and looked at her watch. Just time to complete the reports. She took the books that had been delivered from the various wards, went through them carefully, and wrote her own report. By the time the senior nursing officer arrived she was able to give a comprehensive report from all the wards and had on her desk the pile of Casualty cards showing injuries and treatment received, particulars of all the patients who had come in from the bus crash, who had been treated, sent home, or admitted, operated on, or was still under observation.

Mrs. Benson, the senior nursing officer, walked in, handbag and paper under her arm.

"Good morning. You've had quite a night, I heard on the way up," she said pleasantly.

Marion Hughes nodded. "I'm all ready for you, though. I must say everything went quite smoothly."

"Good." Mrs. Benson nodded her satisfaction, and both women sat down to go through the report books.

When they had finished Marion Hughes got up and put her hand to her forehead.

"Headache?" asked the senior nursing officer.

"Yes. I think it was the heat in Casualty last night. I'll go down to the kitchen and see if I can get a cup of tea and take a couple of aspirins before I go home."

The S.N.O. nodded.

"I should," she said and then added, "By the way, they've laid on some coffee and sandwiches in the canteen for anybody who wants it. I met Sir James coming up and told him, and he said he thought he'd avail himself of the offer, as his operating list begins at nine thirty." She looked at Marion Hughes enquiringly.

"You can get a cup of coffee there, or would you rather have it up here?"

Marion Hughes shook her head. "No, I'll pop into the canteen," she answered. The thought of seeing Sir James Hatfield again now that she was looking her usual fresh self appealed to her. She picked up her handbag and left the office.

On her way downstairs she opened her bag to check if she had any aspirin, found the small bottle that she usually carried with her, and shook two aspirins out into her hand. She went down the stairs that led to the canteen, pushed open the doors, and walked in and looked round. For this time in the morning it was quite crowded. She saw Sir James Hatfield over by the counter, eating a sandwich, a cup of coffee in front of him. She looked round vaguely, noticing that Mrs. Upton was still in the canteen, although it was past her time for going off duty. She saw Marion Hughes and poured her a cup of coffee and brought it over to the table. Marion Hughes nodded a brief thanks as Mrs. Upton put it down in front of her.

As Mrs. Upton put down the coffee, the phone began to ring in the kitchen, and a moment later a maroon-coated cleaner came out through the swing doors, wiping her hands on a rather grubby tea-towel. She came up to Miss Hughes.

"I'm sorry, Miss Hughes, but that was Mrs. Benson. She said if you were still here would I ask you to pop back to the office. There's something she wants to ask about one of the Casualty cards. That's what she said."

Mrs. Upton came fussily back to the table. "Shall I take that away and bring you another cup when you come down?" she said, putting her hand towards the cup and saucer on the table in front of Marion Hughes, who had now stood up.

"No, no, leave it there," said Marion Hughes almost irritably. "It doesn't matter. I won't be a minute. Leave it."

Mrs. Upton, ready to go home, recognized the usual signs of irritability and answered quickly, "All right, Miss Hughes. I was only suggesting . . . Don't be too long, or it will be cold." She gave a meaning look at the still hovering cleaner, and they went back into the kitchen together.

Marion Hughes went out of the canteen, through the swing doors, and rather wearily back to the office.

"So sorry to bring you back, Hughes," said the S.N.O. "It was just a small omission on one of the Casualty cards." She handed the card to Marion Hughes, who took it with a slight gesture of annoyance.

"Oh, I remember this patient, he wasn't badly hurt. He was sent home." Marion Hughes didn't bother to sit down but filled the card in with her rapid, neat writing and handed it to the S.N.O.

"Thanks. Sorry again to bring you back," said Mrs. Benson, and Marion nodded, unsmiling. Her headache now was beginning to make her feel slightly sick, and she turned, left the office, and went back to the canteen. The cup of cooling coffee was standing beside her handbag where she had left it. She momentarily chided herself for leaving her handbag there. It was a thing she would not normally do; probably her headache was making her forgetful. The coffee was cool but warm enough to take two aspirins with. She stirred in some sugar and popped the aspirins into her mouth and drained the cup of coffee, then got up, looked once again round the canteen. Some of the night staff had gone. She looked across to where Sir James Hatfield had been, but his place was vacant and she wondered idly if he had gone home or up to the rest-room. She looked at her watch; twenty to nine. It would soon be time for him to start operating again. Quite a day for him, she thought. He might let Denton start the list for him and put his private patients off until later. He'd probably have to; he wouldn't like that.

She left the canteen slowly, walked down the stairs, out of the front door of the hospital, and into the cool air, with a feeling of thankfulness that the night was over. It had tired her more than she realized, but the aspirin wouldn't take long to ease her headache, and the fresh air was already helping it.

She walked slowly across the asphalt courtyard to where her car was parked and got in. She opened her bag again, felt around for her car key, put the key in the ignition, and sat for a moment; she certainly did feel tired. She thought about her remark to Nigel Denton and his guilty reaction. She half smiled at herself and wondered how he could fit into her scheme of things. She started the car.

Her feeling of tiredness increased, but she backed the car expertly out of her parking space and through the gate of the courtyard.

Yes, she was certainly tired. She would be glad to lead a more restful life. Of course, if she could catch Sir James, as Lady Hatfield she would have to do some entertaining and run a large house, but that would not be as rigorous as nursing and certainly not as tiring as St. Jude's night superintendent. She felt really exhausted. I'm not as young as I was, she thought ruefully, and turned her car into the road that led along by the river towards her flat.

The canteen began to empty, as those engaged in last night's casualty work left, after their unusual bonus of free coffee and sandwiches. Hiram Jones, followed by Atkins, then Nigel Denton and Miss Creasey, until the only one left, sitting immobile at one of the tables, was Staff Carmichael, her cup of coffee untouched in front of her. She was staring across the canteen at nothing, mechanically pulling to pieces a tissue in her hand, rolling it into small pellets, and dropping them on the table. Suddenly she arrived at the last piece of tissue and appeared to awake, as she looked round the now almost deserted canteen, and got hastily to her feet and followed the others.

The sun, once more, slightly bleak and uncertain, shone down on St. Jude's façade.

Of the various casualties who had been admitted the night before, some were now recovering, some were waiting for operations, some for discharge home. The hospital in the early morning had buzzed with the conversation of night staff to day staff. They told each other how much had gone on the night before, how well everything had run. Exaggerated rumours, as usual, flew thick and fast as to the number of casualties, the state of the casualties, and how those who had dealt with the casualties had behaved. It was, for the time being, a nine days' wonder but, as always in hospital circles, contained in itself.

More work, of course, was caused by the influx of patients, and the theatre list made a little awry, because some of the casualties were still to be operated on, and the day staff wished they could have been done in the night rather than interrupting their day list.

The switchboard, too, was busier, because there were enquiries from relatives asking about accident victims as well as the routine enquiries of the morning. But as the day grew a little older, and the sun a little stronger, the fifteen or so admitted casualties became part of the routine of the day, and St. Jude's settled down to its normal routine.

When Hiram Jones arrived home, he felt curiously cold and detached—detached even from John, who emerged from the shower with a large bath towel wrapped round him as he entered the flat.

"Any dope?" he asked Hiram immediately, without even a "Good morning," or a "Had a decent night?" Hiram handed him the manilla envelope and hardly reacted to John's screech of disgust as he saw what it contained.

"Twenty—only twenty. What the bloody hell has happened to the bottleful you promised me? Take it yourself?"

"No, it's gone—vanished out of my pocket," Hiram said and sank tiredly onto the kitchen chair.

"A likely story, I must say." John's voice grated on Hiram's ears as he turned away from him, resting his elbow on the back of the chair. He didn't want to look at John, didn't want to argue or protest.

"What have you done? Hidden the bottle, I suppose. Going to dole me out a few at a time, keeping me on my toes, lover boy." John's face, red from the shower, went redder still.

"You know me better than that," answered Hiram quietly. He felt too tired, too shaken, to carry on the row. He got up and went into the bedroom, closed the door, and sat down on the bed, his head in his hands. John burst into the bedroom after him.

"You'll have to do better than this, if you want to keep me, Hiram. I'm not kidding." John stood over him and Hiram didn't even look up. He knew only too well what John's face would look like.

"You don't know what I've done for you already, John," answered Hiram. "Please, leave me alone."

"I'll do that—no danger," answered John and slammed the door behind him and left Hiram alone.

The next night Hiram was the first to arrive for night duty. This was unusual. He usually just scraped up to the ward in time to get the report, scrambling himself into his uniform coat. Tonight he was early, and he was worried. Before going to Stenton ward, he had decided to go into Casualty and ask if anything had been found. He would not be specific, and perhaps the nurse might say, "Well, we did find a bottle of Nembutal." He could claim it, he supposed, say he had been to the chemist and cashed a prescription for a friend.

He hoped it wouldn't be Casualty sister on duty, only a staff nurse, or even a junior. He made his way into the department and swore softly to himself as he saw who was in charge. It was Sister, a stiff, stern, older woman.

"Oh, Sister, I wonder if you could help me," he said.

"If I can, Nurse." She looked at her watch. "You're on early. Aren't you on Stenton ward, night Staff Nurse?"

Hiram nodded. "Yes, Sister, but last night we were all here in Casualty."

"Yes, you had quite a night, didn't you? You didn't leave everything too tidy either," Sister answered.

"Oh, I'm sorry about that, Sister," said Hiram lamely.

"Well, I suppose it's only to be expected. You're not used to the place. What is it you want me to help you with?"

"I lost something here last night."

"You lost something, in the department, in Casualty?" Sister looked up at him, puzzled.

"I put my uniform coat in the cloakroom and put on a plastic apron. You see . . ." Hiram swallowed hard. "There was a bottle in the pocket of my coat. When I went to get it back in the morning, it had gone."

"The coat or the bottle?" said Sister, looking at him directly.

"No, just the bottle. My coat was still there," said Hiram.

"Well, you shouldn't bring alcoholic drinks on duty. What was it: whisky, brandy, what?"

"It was brandy," said Hiram quickly. "I wasn't feeling very well. I just brought it down with me. I wondered, had you found it?"

Sister looked at him oddly. "No, we certainly haven't found a bottle, or not that I know of. I'll ask Nurse."

"Oh, please don't bother," said Hiram.

"It's no bother," said Sister mildly. She put her hand up and a nurse walking past in the Casualty area saw the raised hand through the glass window of Sister's office and came in.

"Yes, Sister," she said.

"Nurse, Staff Jones here was in Casualty last night from the geriatric ward, helping, and he lost a—" She looked at Hiram sideways and went on, "He lost a bottle from his uniform coat pocket. The coat was hanging in cloaks. You haven't seen it, have you?"

"A bottle?" said the nurse, looking at Hiram and giving a slight smile. "No." She shook her head.

"All right, Nurse, thank you. I thought you would have told me if you had. Sorry, Nurse Jones. If anything turns up I'll let you know, but you shouldn't bring things like that. You shouldn't carry that sort of thing with you, indeed. It wouldn't be a full bottle, would it?" she asked.

"Oh no, it was only a tiny little brown plastic bottle. I just put some in, you see," said Hiram.

"I see. Ward brandy, was it?" Sister looked up at him again.

"Well, I shouldn't make a habit of doing that," she said, then returned to writing her day report for the night casualty staff nurse, who would soon be on duty.

"Thank you, Sister. May I just look in the cloakroom?" asked Hiram. "Please."

"Do, if you want to," said Sister, not looking up again.

Hiram hurried out of Casualty, through into the waiting-room, and into the cloakroom. He looked round, underneath where his overall had hung, on the window ledges, and in the shoe cupboard, which smelled of tired, sweaty feet. The bottle was nowhere.

Someone had pinched it. Someone who liked Nembutal and didn't care how they got it. Who? The changing room last night had been milling with doctors, nurses, porters, changing into their plastic aprons, changing back again. It was hopeless to try and pinpoint anybody. He hadn't even a suspicion.

Now he had to cope with Mr. Butterworth and John. Old Butterworth might have found out by now that the pills were missing. He'd have to give him two every night now to keep him quiet, or he'd say he'd had some pills brought in. He'd tell everybody who would listen. He'd say that Hiram had asked him to have them brought in.

Suddenly another idea flashed across Hiram's mind. Could Marion Hughes herself have found them? Gone into the cloakroom during the night, during all that activity, to go to the loo, or powder her nose, knocked against his coat and then seen the bottle. Could she have taken it? She'd recognize Mr. Butterworth's name on the label, put two and two together. Well, in that case . . . He left the cloakroom and Casualty and went up to Stenton ward.

When he got to the ward Hiram felt shaken and listened to the day report almost without hearing it, not that it varied much.

At last the geriatric ward sister closed the book and left. The day staff called out good night and disappeared up the corridor and down the stairs, and Hiram walked into the kitchen.

"Good God, what's the matter with you? I thought you'd look better after a day's rest," his junior said. "You look terrible, white as a sheet. Was last night too much for you?"

"No, I'm all right. Just had a bit of a shock, that's all."

"I'll make you some tea, dearie," said Atkins. "John not been playing you up again, has he?"

"What do you know about John? Why do you always keep mentioning him? What does anyone know about John?" said Hiram dully.

"Oh, quite a bit, dear, don't you worry. You can't do much in this place without everybody knowing about it," said his junior, filling the kettle at the sink and raising his voice above the splashing of the water. "Nobody can have an affair, or pinch a couple of ward sheets, or make a mistake in taking a temperature, you name it, you'll hear about it. It's because it's such a small place, you see. Sometimes I hate it," said Atkins, banging the kettle down on the stove. "I don't believe I'm born to this kind of life. I can't stand the constant yacking on about each other that goes on."

"Well, you're not exactly backward at doing it yourself," said Hiram bitterly.

"I know, I know, Staff, that's just it. I wasn't like this when I came, I was really quite a nice lad. Anyway, cheer up, it can't be as bad as all that. Wait till Hughesie comes round, that'll put your mind back in perspective, that'll make you see the real horrors of the night." Atkins chortled on.

Hiram sat down at the table and had a cup of tea. He felt

sick at the thought of trying to explain to old Butterworth what had happened to his pills, if he had found out by now that they were missing. He finished drinking the tea moodily. His junior nurse looked at him sympathetically. He got up and went off into the ward.

Nigel Denton, doing his ten o'clock round, came to the children's ward. This round was almost a formality: asking the nurse in charge if everything was all right, looking at the patients who had been lately operated on. This evening it had been a little busier, for there had been last night's casualties, some of them recently out of theatre to check and order medication for, but on the children's ward there was no one from last night's accident. Nevertheless there was one small child whose appendix he had removed late in the afternoon, and he wanted to see that all was satisfactory.

He walked quietly into the middle of the ward where Carmichael was sitting writing. "Everything all right, Nurse?" he asked. She looked up at him, her face white and strained, but then, he reflected, it usually was.

"I've just come to see that kid I operated on at four o'clock. All right, is he?" He tried to sound reassuring, casual.

Carmichael looked down at the report and found the child's entry. She nodded. "Yes, he was perfectly all right when the day staff went off and seems so now." She got up and, walking beside Nigel, came down to the end bed where the child lay. The little boy was sleeping quietly, his face flushed, a little perspiration making his dark hair stick to his forehead. He stirred a little as they stood there, whimpered quietly, and then sank back into sleep.

"He's had a sedative?" Nigel asked.

Carmichael nodded. "He looks all right, wasn't much of an appendix really, slightly inflamed, that's all, but better out."

Nigel went to the side of the cot, looking more closely at the child, took hold of the small wrist, felt the pulse, and nodded. "He's all right, but keep an eye on him."

"Of course." Nurse Carmichael sounded almost hostile.

"I didn't mean . . ." Nigel smiled and as they walked out of the ward tried to make light conversation. It wasn't easy with Carmichael.

"You did well in the Casualty last night. Makes a change from the children's ward, eh? Quite a night, wasn't it? Everybody did very well, I thought."

"Did you? Well, Miss Hughes certainly didn't think I did very well," said Nurse Carmichael, and her voice shook.

"Oh, I'm sorry. What did you do wrong?" Nigel looked at her widely dilated pupils as they stared up at him.

"I was there. I shouldn't have been. Good night, Mr. Denton," she answered coldly and walked away from him into the nursery.

Oh dear, Nigel thought, old Hughes even made trouble in that set-up did she? I thought Carmichael was really proving herself quite efficient. Wonder what she did wrong? Poor little devil. He thought suddenly of Marion Hughes's remark about smelling drink on people's breath and grimaced and made his way towards the Common Room.

He opened the door to find George Hayward sitting comfortably in one of the chairs, watching television.

"Anything good on?" asked Nigel.

"Not that you'd notice," said George. "Makes a change. Have a beer?" He indicated a six pack beside him. "Went over to the pub and fetched them," he said. "Good ale, that."

"Thanks," said Nigel. He opened a can and drank and bumped down into the chair beside George Hayward.

"Just been to the children's ward. I thought Carmichael,

that staff nurse with the peaky face, you know, acquitted herself well last night, but according to her she didn't. She and
Hughes must have had a row of some kind. Carmichael looks
pretty shattered."

"Well, it would be difficult to acquit yourself well with
Marion," answered George without much interest. He turned
suddenly, as if remembering something.

"By the way, she hasn't turned up tonight," he said.

"Hasn't turned up?" Nigel's hand gripping the can of beer
tightened visibly, so that the knuckles showed white.

"That's right, quite a mystery," said George. "There was
the S.N.O. apparently, waiting in her office, so the story goes;
nothing happened, and it's now," he glanced at his watch,
"twenty to twelve, mate, and I've not heard that she's turned
up yet."

Nigel put the beer down on the table in front of him, as if
he'd suddenly lost the taste for it. "It's not like her. She's
probably been taken ill, 'flu or something."

"She's got a phone, but apparently nobody's heard anything," said George.

"Well . . ." Nigel's voice sounded strangely hesitant.
"Probably her car broke down."

"It wouldn't dare," said George.

It soon became common knowledge in the hospital that the
night superintendent hadn't reported for duty. It was greeted
with various degrees of puzzlement, not untinged with the joy
that her absence usually created.

"Well, I heard," said one nurse, hanging up her cloak in the
Casualty cloakroom, "that she'd been brought into Intensive
Care with a brain haemorrhage."

"Never, I don't believe it, she's too young for that, isn't she?" said her companion.

"Not at all, it can happen at any time," said the other. She whisked into Casualty to report on duty.

This rumour had no doubt come from someone who had heard Miss Hughes say that she'd got a headache.

In the operating-theatre, Sir James was working late. He was operating on a private patient for varicose veins and was not in a very good temper. He had found that because of last night's accident the theatre had been annexed by the Ortho-pod. Therefore he'd had to put his operation off until now.

Both he and Dr. Galbraith, who was anaesthetizing for him, would not have done this if it had not been for the exceptional circumstances of the bus crash, the fact that all three theatres had been involved, and of course the fee.

"What's the time, Nurse?" he said suddenly, the electric theatre clock was behind him.

"Half-past eleven, sir; well twenty-past," said the nurse.

"Oh, then Miss Hughes will be on," said Sir James and went on tying off the veins.

"Oh, no, Sir James, she's not reported for duty for some reason. I don't think they can find out why." The junior nurse spoke up importantly; the night theatre sister was off duty and Sir James was being assisted by the staff nurse, so the junior felt she could speak more freely.

"Not reported for duty?" said Sir James.

"No, sir, she just hasn't turned up, that's all," said the nurse, glad to be able to report new information to the great man. "Perhaps, sir, she's had an accident," she went on.

"Nothing trivial, I hope," said Sir James. Dr. Galbraith

looked up sharply from his perusal of the *British Medical Journal.*

The nurse did a giggle behind her hand and turned away. The staff nurse on the other side of the theatre table raised her eyes to Sir James in astonishment. Sir James's and Galbraith's eyes met, and Sir James made a gesture as much as to say—I shouldn't have said that, it just slipped out. Both men nodded to each other, ignoring the nurses and the operation proceeded.

Hiram Jones, still preoccupied, terrified by the loss of his bottle of capsules, still thinking where it might be and who might have it, listened to his junior when he came back into the kitchen. Atkins's eyes were wide with astonishment.

"She's not turned up, old Hughesie. Funny, you know, a porter's just told me in the corridor. The S.N.O. was waiting there apparently, to give the report, and well, well, she just didn't come. Funny . . ."

Hiram stood there. His face went even whiter than it had been before, and he looked at Atkins as if he had been struck dumb. Then suddenly he stammered, "Wh-wh-what did you say . . . wh-what?" He sat down heavily on the kitchen chair.

"Old Hughesie's not turned up. For goodness' sake, I thought you'd be delighted. I thought it would make your night," said his junior.

"Miss Hughes . . . ?" Hiram didn't seem to be taking it in.

"Well, she hasn't come, I can tell you that. The S.N.O. was waiting, getting a bit wild, I should think. She waited until about ten-past nine and then decided to give the report to the junior night superintendent, old Norman. Thank God for that, I say; we'll have a bit of a beano tonight. I'll do a fry-up if you like."

Hiram didn't answer, just sat staring in front of him.

"Having trouble again are we, with John, I mean?" Nurse Atkins went on.

"No, I'm not, just keep quiet. It's nothing to do with you," said Hiram sharply, almost hysterically.

"Oh, all right, don't get shirty; don't be like that," said his junior. "Anyway John was here last night, looking for you, but of course you were so busy, so important, coping with the casualties and all that, I told him he'd best not go near you."

"John?" Hiram turned his white, startled face towards Atkins. "John was here last night?"

"Yes, didn't he tell you when he got home this morning?" asked his junior.

"No, he didn't—he didn't say anything about it. Are you sure?" Hiram said.

"I'm telling you, he was here last night. I told him you were in Casualty, and if he went there, he'd run full tilt into dear Marion, Sir James, the lot, so I suppose he kept out of the way and I don't blame him." Atkins looked again at Hiram's face, shrugged his shoulders, and went back into the ward.

Hiram clenched his hands together and beat his closed fists softly against his forehead. Was that where the bottle had gone? It must be. But how would he know that I'd hang my coat up in the cloakroom in Casualty? Well, he could have gone through and recognized my coat—after all it's got my name on it. Then he'd take the bottle. Still, at least he'd know enough not to take a fatal dose. Hiram felt as if his heart had stopped beating and yet partly relieved. At least he knew, or was almost sure he knew, where the bottle had gone. The envelope—well John hadn't discovered that when he'd discovered the bottle. If John had got the bottle, those pills weren't running round the hospital for some barmy patient to swallow, that was something.

There was only old Butterworth to deal with now.

Hiram gave out the night medicines from the trolley, and when he arrived at Mr. Butterworth's bed, he felt again that faint, dreadful feeling.

"Pills for me tonight, got me pills?" said Mr. Butterworth, looking slyly up at Hiram.

"Yes, got two for you tonight," said Hiram, hastily putting the two capsules in the old man's hand and giving him the small medicine glass full of water with which to take them. He watched him put the capsules in his mouth and swallow them down with the water and waited to see if he was going to speak again and say anything about the bottle of Nembutal being missing, but he didn't. He settled down quite cosily in his bed and said, "Can I have me pee bottle by me bed? I'll put the sheet over it so nobody will see it."

Hiram nodded absently, thankful that the old man had apparently not discovered that his precious bottle of capsules was missing. But how long would it be before he did?

As he wheeled the medicine trolley out of the ward, he stopped by Nurse Atkins, who was changing an old man's disposable draw sheet.

"I've got to make a phone call. Will you put these medicines away?" said Hiram.

"Okey-doke," said his junior. "Will do."

Hiram went down to the communal phone that was situated at the junction of four corridors leading to four wards. He dialled his home number and waited. After a time—it seemed an age—John answered.

"John, you were here last night again. Atkins told me. You were looking for me. What did you want?"

"A few pills, of course. I haven't had enough lately. You've brought home hardly any, and you said you'd get a bottleful for me, didn't you—remember? I went out with a lovely fellow today. He's got a much better supply than yours. Works in a chemist's actually."

"John, did you take that bottle of pills out of the pocket of my uniform in the cloakroom off the Casualty waiting-room?"

"What are you talking about? Of course I didn't," said John.

"You were here; you must have taken them. They were in a bottle, a little plastic bottle. You haven't met anyone who comes from a chemist's. You took those pills, and . . . You don't know what it cost me to get those pills, and I've been nearly out of my mind all day because the bottle had gone. I found the bottle was missing when I came to pick up my coat after working in Casualty last night. I feel dreadful. Come on, tell me the truth, please."

"I don't know what you're talking about." There was a ring of truth in John's voice. "I haven't seen any beastly old bottle. I did put my head round the Casualty door, but there was far too much gore about for me to come in. I didn't see you, anyway. I only saw dear Miss Hughes and lots of bods lying about. I thought I'd better beat it, so I did. I don't know what you're accusing me of. I must go now, off to bed. I'm worn out this evening."

"John, I beg you to tell me the truth," pleaded Hiram.

"I've told you the truth. I've not touched your old bottle," said John and put the phone down with a crash.

Hiram put the phone down at his end. He didn't know whether to believe John or not. If John had come to Casualty last night he might have taken them. It was dangerous this visiting the hospital. He'd have to stop John doing it. Yet he felt only relief at the thought of the capsules with John, at least safe. He hadn't met anyone from a chemist, John hadn't. That was just too much of a coincidence. As Hiram walked away from the phone, doubts began to creep in again. John didn't often lie. But no, he must have them, he must. His luck about the whole thing seemed to be holding. If John had got them, it was only the problem now of old Butterworth finding out they had gone, and another day just couldn't go by without the old man discovering they weren't there. Hiram sighed. There were so many problems; his mind buzzed with them. If Butterworth found out tomorrow they'd gone, well, he'd hear about it as soon as he came on duty, and for the moment he'd have to dismiss it from his mind and get on with his work. At least the old chap had taken his two Nembutals and would sleep the night through. He wouldn't be searching round for the bottle just to check it was there, at least till tomorrow, and even then he might not.

Then there was Hughes . . . Marion Hughes . . . Hiram shut his mind off with a click like a camera shutter and went back to the ward.

The night passed uneventfully. It was only when Mrs. Benson, the senior nursing officer, came on in the morning and received the report from Miss Norman that any real anxiety was voiced about Marion Hughes.

"You've heard nothing? She didn't phone or anything?" she asked. "Nothing?"

"Nothing, nothing at all," answered Miss Norman. "To tell you the truth, I phoned her flat again last night but there was no reply."

"So did I. I hope there's nothing wrong," said the senior nursing officer.

"How could there be? Perhaps she's gone to bed with a temperature and doesn't feel like answering the phone," said Miss Norman. "But you would have expected her to let us know by now, get a neighbour to phone or something."

"Yes. She lives in a flat, doesn't she? There must be some-one else she could ask."

"I don't know though," said Miss Norman frankly. "She's not a very friendly soul. I mean, I expect she keeps herself to herself," she amended hastily. "Perhaps the neighbours . . . well . . ."

"Yes." The S.N.O. looked at her watch. "It's twenty to nine now. If she hasn't phoned, well, by ten o'clock, I think we ought to go round to her flat. Someone ought to anyway."

"That's a good idea," said Miss Norman and gave a rather obvious yawn.

"I don't mean you," said Miss Benson. "I think I'll go round myself. I wonder—I suppose she couldn't have . . ."

"Couldn't have what?" asked Miss Norman.

"Well, had a brain haemorrhage or something like that."

"Good Lord, funny you should say that. That's the rumour that was going round last night. It all stemmed from someone saying she was complaining of a headache when she left."

"Well, I hope it's nothing like that. If it is, I wonder should we . . ." The senior nursing officer looked suddenly serious and thoughtful. "Don't worry, you go home. The moment it's nine o'clock I know Miss Hogg will be there and I'll ring her up. After all, it's the chief nursing officer's job to sort out problems like this. If she wants me to go round to Marion's flat, I'll go, but she'll probably be back tonight saying that she had a migraine or something and her phone was out of order."

The junior night superintendent nodded. "I'm off," she said. "The whole mystery will no doubt be cleared up by tonight and Marion Hughes will be back on duty as good as new. Bye-bye." She went out of the office with a thankful straightening of the shoulders and made her way out of the hospital to get a good day's rest.

Mrs. Benson, the S.N.O., toyed with the phone, running her fingers up and down the receiver in its cradle. The bell pinged as she did it, and she withdrew her hand.

"Shall I ring Miss Hogg? Suppose I'll have to," she said aloud. Then she shrugged impatiently as her thoughts went on . . . Silly bitch, why on earth didn't she let us know if she couldn't get in? Surely she could have got someone to ring up even if she is ill, a friend, but then knowing her I doubt if she's got any. She makes enough trouble when she's here and more when she's away. She looked at her watch again—two minutes past nine. She picked up the phone and dialled. She would ask the indomitable Miss Hogg, chief nursing officer, what she should do, and suggest that perhaps it might be a good idea if she went round to Marion Hughes's flat to see if she was there, or if she'd been taken ill, or at least to try and find out somehow why she had not appeared for duty last night. It was so unlike her.

In answer the chief nursing officer's efficient voice suggested, as she had thought, that she go round to Miss Hughes's flat straightaway, got the caretaker to let her in, and then report back to her at her office.

Miss Hogg played with the end of her pen reflectively and looked up at her S.N.O. "And there was nothing, nothing to suggest that she'd gone away?"

"No. I got the key from the caretaker in the basement flat after a little argument. She let me in because I said it was a case of emergency. I took the liberty of opening Miss Hughes's wardrobe but I can't tell if any clothes have been taken. There were two suitcases there, but she may have more. I asked about the car. It's usually parked out in the front—there's a space for each flat—but it wasn't there, and there was another car in its place."

"That's odd. Has she . . . said anything about anyone she might have? Well, she's a little old to elope, but you know what I mean." Miss Hogg looked tentatively up at Mrs. Benson.

The S.N.O. shook her head. "No indeed, she's an attractive woman, but I've never heard her mention a man friend or a date. But she wouldn't if I know Marion Hughes, she wouldn't tell anyone anything. She keeps most things to herself, except her complaints about the staff."

"I know. She does drive people a bit, doesn't she?" said the C.N.O. discreetly. "But she's an extremely efficient manager and this I think was shown the night before last at that Casualty . . . You don't think that had any bearing on it, do you? You don't think she was under more pressure than we realized?" the chief nursing officer went on.

"Well, as I told you, she did complain of this headache, and when she didn't come I wondered, stupidly perhaps, if she'd been taken ill in her flat."

"Was she prone to tension headaches?"

"I don't know." The S.N.O. sounded slightly weary. "I really don't know. She'd never complained to me before."

Miss Hogg nodded. "Well, I hate to say this, but I'd better go and see the hospital secretary and see what he says. If she's disappeared completely I suppose we ought to report it, but a grown person can take off if she likes, there's no law against it. It's just the inconvenience, and the fact that it's so out of character. I'll talk to him. You go back to St. Jude's. I'll see to it.

"I doubt he'll go to the police. After all it's rather stupid, isn't it? Going to say a thirty-eight- . . ." She stopped, then continued, ". . . year-old woman is missing in her car. We may have to give it a day or two, I don't know. After all it was early morning when she went off. It's not likely that . . ." She stopped, her thoughts obviously wandering round the problem.

"Still you do hear things don't you? People are found after being . . . Well I'll deal with it," said the C.N.O. firmly.

Mrs. Benson left the office to go back to her own hospital, to her own duties, and, she hoped, no more problems.

There would of course be a slight problem tonight. Norman would just have to take over the hospital again. But she seemed to take charge so easily, and the hospital seemed to run just as smoothly as when Marion Hughes was on. With these more cheerful thoughts the S.N.O. got into her car and drove back to St. Jude's.

Hiram arrived home determined to put John through a third degree, if necessary, just to put his mind at rest. Those capsules had been taken from his overall pocket, and the bottle was here if John had taken it, somewhere in the flat.

John was in when he got home, in the kitchen, cooking bacon and egg.

"Want some?" he called out cheerfully.

"No. Yes, all right, I'll have some," Hiram changed his

mind. The last thing in the world he felt like was eating, but it would give them time to talk if they were both sitting by the kitchen table.

He went through into the bedroom and changed into another sweater. As he pulled it over his head and went back into the kitchen, the smell of bacon and eggs was more appetizing than he'd expected.

"You're in a good mood. What's making you so happy? It's not often you cook breakfast for me," he said to John curiously.

"Felt like it, lovey. Feel nice and relaxed, you know. Had a good night, went to bed early for once."

"And with plenty of Nembutal, slept well," said Hiram and then instantly regretted it as John swung round from the cooking and said,

"Well, you did give me some, you know, but as I told you, this friend of mine, he's not a pharmacist, but he works in a chemist's shop, he may change things quite a bit, so you'd better watch out. No, I didn't have any Nembutal. As a matter of fact, I slept because I was so damned worn out. I've still got what you gave me." He turned back to his cooking and Hiram resolved not to say another word about that subject until they were both sitting down at the table.

"I'll make some coffee," he muttered and proceeded to mix some instant coffee in two mugs with milk powder.

He stirred them both and John took one mug, looked at it, and said, "More coffee than that. I don't like wishy-washy stuff."

Automatically Hiram added more coffee to the mixture and stirred it. He put the sugar basin on the table and the two mugs of coffee. By that time John had the bacon and eggs on two plates and had plonked them down on the table as well. He took a handful of cutlery out of the drawer and put that on the table in a heap.

"Help yourself. I'm not a butler, you know," he said and turned back to the grill and withdrew two pieces of toast, which he put down beside the plates.

Hiram got up and took two small plates from the stove and put one in front of John, picking the toast up from the table and placing it on the plate.

"Oh, pernickety, shall I get some paper napkins? Are we living graciously today?" said John and grinned. The grin was half malicious, half affectionate. He was obviously in a good mood. Hiram had got to go carefully to keep it that way.

John attacked his bacon and egg. Hiram toyed with his.

"Who's this friend then? The one who works in the chemist's, I mean," asked Hiram.

"Oh, Jacko," said John. "He's a nice boy, quite one of us, and I think he could be useful."

"John—" Hiram put his hand across the table and covered John's hand, the hand holding the knife, just about to carve through a bit more bacon. "John, please," Hiram said. "You're not thinking of . . . ?"

"Oh, don't get your knickers in a twist," said John. "No, I don't fancy him really." He went on, "I'm going to keep him on the friendly hook, you know what I mean. He might be useful, and after all you don't seem to do so well."

"Those pills, that bottle, did you take it from my overall in Casualty, the night of the bus crash, the night before last?"

"What are you talking about?" John looked genuinely bewildered.

"John, a lot depends on it. I got them for you, but they belong to a patient, and he's going to report that they've disappeared. I must make up some story. I must know where they are. If you've got them, I don't mind a bit, they were for you; but if they're wandering round the hospital, think of it: Nembutal capsules. Supposing a mental patient got hold of them and took the lot. They'd find out. It would be the end of me, truly. Please, please tell me if you took it. At least I'd know where they are."

"I didn't take them. I don't even know what you're talking about, truly I don't." John looked at Hiram's stricken face and obviously realized that he was in a terrible state.

"Look, love," he said. "I came to Casualty, put my head round the door, as I said. There was blood, and God knows what, people sitting there with their heads in their hands, terrible. That chap up on Stenton, he said you were there in Casualty, but I wouldn't come in. I never got past those damned plastic doors, let alone came in to look for your coat. Why should I? You said you'd got some, but I hardly believed you really. No, cross my heart and hope to die, love, I never took any bottle from your pocket. And if I had, what's the point of holding out on you? As you say, you got 'em for me, anyway."

Hiram pushed the plate of bacon and eggs away from him and started breaking the crisp toast into little bits and letting them drop onto the plate.

"I believe you, John. I wish to God you had taken them, but where's that bottle now?" he said.

Sir James left the operating-theatre at about three in the morning. He felt put out. Having to do private patients at night was untoward, unforgivable. He would bring it up at the next Management Committee meeting. Casualties would have to wait until the ordinary lists were finished. He could not ask his private patients to be operated on at that hour, not again; and they shouldn't ask him to do it, it wasn't good enough. Of course, some of the casualties hadn't been able to wait, he knew that, but even so he was put out, thoroughly put out.

He put the Rover away in the garage and went into his house and poured himself the usual whisky. This was getting to be a habit that might have to stop. Madeleine wouldn't perhaps . . . The thought of Madeleine was pleasant, but it put Marion Hughes into his head again.

He shouldn't have said that to Galbraith, stupid thing to say, "Nothing trivial, I hope." It was one of those things that slipped out. He'd meant it, though. It would be a relief to see the back of that woman. Perhaps it wouldn't matter what she said about the child, but to have to explain it all, to Madeleine particularly, or to anyone else, was irksome. He didn't want to have to do it. And then there was the Irish child.

Perhaps that nurse who'd giggled in the theatre when he'd said, "Nothing trivial, I hope," perhaps she'd remember and repeat it to her colleagues.

" 'An accident—nothing trivial I hope.' Sir James said that, can you imagine? He must hate the sight of her, mustn't he?"

That would make rumours rife again. He was a fool. He usually guarded his tongue carefully. He tried to put the whole thing out of his head. He downed the whisky quickly and decided to try and get a few hours' sleep.

He looked at his watch. Five o'clock, for God's sake, and it was his list again in the morning. Well, he'd try and get three hours' sleep at least. He went upstairs, undressed, and got into bed. For a long time he lay looking into the grey dawn, Marion Hughes uppermost in his mind. It was some time before he stopped turning restlessly and fell into an uneasy sleep.

Nigel Denton liked Miss Norman, the junior night superintendent. She was a nice uncomplicated woman, easy to work with. You didn't feel the tension there always was round Marion Hughes; perhaps Marion Hughes was lying on the floor of her flat at this moment, unconscious, he thought. But no, he'd heard vaguely that somebody had been round to the flat to have a look and she hadn't been there, neither had her car. He smiled to himself: well, they would see.

He smiled again as he remembered George Hayward's remark when he had said that her car might have broken down and he had answered, "It wouldn't dare." That was true, he thought. Nothing, nobody, must break down as far as the night super was concerned.

He remembered her remarks about the smell of drink on the breath. Her obvious recollection of his wife's death that night the young stripper had been in Casualty. Yes, a nasty piece of work. People might wonder why she hadn't turned up, but he hadn't met one person who'd been really concerned. Well, that's the way of it, he thought. The lady vanishes and nobody cares a lot. They just wonder.

The river running through Woollton was polluted by the various effluents that the factories allowed to escape into the water. By law they were forbidden to do this; nevertheless, it still happened. Water ran turbid and thick like soup between the factories on one side and a grass verge on the other which sloped up to the main road.

Two boys sat right on the edge of the river, dangling homemade fishing rods in the water. "We'll never catch any fish here. My Dad said they all died years ago."

"Your Dad could be wrong. Grown-ups often are," said the

other, watching his float bob up and down in the murky stream which ran quickly by them.

"Well, I think it's a waste of time. I'd just as soon be at school. I don't see the point of playing hookey for this kind of thing."

"Oh, shut up. I like fishing and you said you did. If we don't catch anything here we'll get a bus and go farther out where it's green and perhaps cleaner."

"Don't be a fathead. It's the same river. Pollution doesn't stop just like that because the banks are green; it goes on. I know. My Dad said so."

"One more word about your Dad," said his companion giving him a punch, "and I'll just about pack it in. If you don't want to stay, go to school, go on."

"How can I go to school now, dafty? It's eleven o'clock," said the other boy.

Resignedly his mate pulled his float out of the water and said, "Come on then; let's try a bit higher up. It may be a bit cleaner. It does look a bit mucky here, but animals adapt themselves to their new surroundings, you know. We had that in that lesson about evolution or something a bit ago."

"Fish aren't animals."

"Oh, yes, they are."

"Oh, no, they're not."

"Oh, yes, they are."

"Oh, no, they're not."

This senseless argument went on as the two boys tramped farther up the river and then settled down again, throwing in their homemade lines, baited with bread. Again one was optimistic, the other showed his obvious boredom. Suddenly, however, he perked up.

"What's that? Look!" he said. "In the middle of the river, over there, what is it, something—look, it shows white . . ."

"It's a car, the top of a car. Gee, fancy dumping your car in the river to get rid of it. My Dad says it costs money to have your car taken away if it's a wreck, so people dump them anywhere in the country, but I've never heard of one being dumped in a river," said his friend.

They withdrew their lines again and chucked them down on the river bank and walked along and sat opposite the object in the middle of the river.

"Look, I don't reckon it was dumped. I reckon it came off the road by mistake. Look." He pointed, and there on the grass ridge that ran between the road and the river bank were tyre marks.

"Well, if they dumped it they'd have to drive it in. I mean at night, wouldn't they?"

"I dunno. Supposing there's somebody in it?" Their eyes grew round with delighted horror.

"A murder, you mean?"

"No, just an accident, drove off the road, you know. I mean it could have happened in the night, or early morning, sometime when there weren't many cars about, nobody would see it. It just went in, and . . . We ought to tell the police."

"They don't take any notice, and we're playing hookey. That's going to be nice, isn't it? We'd better do nothing about it." He gazed at the top of the car with interest, as it gently disappeared again under the water.

"It's floating; the river's deep here, you know. There was a chap drowned once, do you remember?"

His friend nodded. "That's why nobody noticed it, I suppose; not that anybody looks down here." He looked across at the blank wall of the factory.

"Perhaps we should tell someone. We'd better go and tell . . ." the other said uncertainly.

"How about telling your Dad or mine?"

"They're at work, aren't they? No, we'd better go to the police station."

"They won't believe us. I told you, they never believe anything we say."

"I bet they will, and I think we ought to do it. Perhaps there's someone in that car." The boy's voice rose slightly hysterically. "Come on," he said, and they both turned and scrambled up the grass bank and ran along the main road, back into Woollton. Something had gripped them both, a fear that was greater than what would happen to them because they'd stayed away from school. They'd got to tell someone.

"There's a car in the river, up by Winton's, you know Winton's the carpet factory. There's a car there in the river, a white car, floating." The boys gasped it out at the police station.

"Now, wait a minute, young sirs," said the policeman behind the desk. "Just give me your names and addresses, both of you."

Speaking together, admonished by the policeman, panting because they'd run all the way to the station, trying to avoid answering when the policeman said mildly, "Why aren't you both in school?" the story came out. The car, might be someone in it, tyre marks on the grass verge. The policeman took it all down patiently and meticulously. He said, "Now you sit down a minute and I'll make a call."

He disappeared through into the back office. Two more men joined him. The door was shut firmly and the boys could not guess what was going on. Suddenly the desk sergeant emerged.

"Right," he said. "Off you go now. We've got your names and addresses. If we want you any more we'll call you. You'd better get off to school, where you should be."

"We can't go back to school now. The morning's nearly over. We'll have to get a note from Mum, about a cold or something," said one. The other nodded and the policeman raised his eyes to heaven.

"Think we should go back to the river?" one boy asked the other.

"Not half. We might miss something, you never know. If they're fishing up that car, there might be a body in it—more than one, perhaps four."

"Yea," the other nodded. "But I don't know that I want to see bodies. Do you?"

"Yes," said the other positively. "I jolly well do, just like the Sweeney and all that."

"All right then," said the other. "We'll go back."

At the river there was already a great deal of activity, with two police cars parked just above the grass verge in the road opposite where the car could be seen. A policeman was measuring the tyre tracks down to the river. Another seemed to be taking an impression of one of the tracks, which thrilled the boys.

"Just like on telly," said one. The other nodded.

"Come on. Let's go nearer and watch."

There were one or two people already there. As they stood and watched, a large crane drove up the path beside the river.

"They're going to pick it up. Look, that's a grabber."

"Great. I know where that comes from. It comes from where they break the cars up, you know." The other boy nodded again. "I've always wanted to see this; the water comes pouring out of the car, and then—"

The crane manoeuvred itself into position on the pathway where the boys had so recently been fishing. There was just room to take the great vehicle. The growing crowd of people seemed to sense that something was happening. They waited and waited. After what seemed a long time—a few people had already left, getting cold by the chilly river—the arm of the

crane centred over the submerged car. Then the grab was
lowered, and after a few fruitless clutches the crane driver
managed to fit it firmly over the car top.

It began to rise from the water. Turbid, dirty, slushy mud
poured from under the doors, just as the boy had predicted
and had seen on television. Higher and higher the crane
swung until the driver looked across and nodded to the police,
then manoeuvred the crane sideways, and the car was swung
over the grass verge, above the road, and was gently, gently
lowered. Even when the tyres touched the road surface, the
water didn't stop pouring from the side of the car, and the
onlookers pressed forward with interest and a certain amount
of enjoyment. This, as the boys said, was better than telly.
This was for real.

The bottom of the car was covered with mud, but the top
looked as if it had just been washed; it shone in the springtime
sunshine. It landed with a soft plop on the road as the crane
driver lowered it. Then, in his cab, he manoeuvred the great
grab, released the car, and swung away. The engine of the
crane stopped, and the driver scrambled out and up the small
grass slope in his heavy wellingtons.

The policemen stood around the car now, and the boys
scrambled up the bank to be near. Although the police were
saying, "Get back, stand back, please. Nothing here to see.
Come along now, get moving," nobody moved away.

A policeman went to the door on the driver's side, turned
the handle, and the door swung open. There was a gasp from
the crowd: it had been well worth waiting for, for there sitting
in the driver's seat, slumped slightly forward, slightly sideways,
and covered with a dirty, slimy ooze, was a body.

"Oo-er, there's someone in it, look," a voice said.

"Can't see if it's a man or a woman from here," said another.

The crowd murmured half in horror, half in appreciation.

An ambulance came up the road, its siren wailing, and stopped beside the drenched car.

A stretcher. The body of Marion Hughes was gently placed on it. Her face, her hair, her suit, her neat shoes and stockings were all in place but covered with the brown slime.

"Won't know who it is till it's had a good hose down," said someone in the crowd, and there was an assenting murmur.

"That's enough now. Nothing else to see. Please move along," said one of the young policemen, and the thing on the stretcher was slid into the ambulance, and the doors were closed. The ambulance men hopped inside the front of the ambulance, no one in the back with Marion Hughes, there was no need for that. They drove off, sirens wailing again.

The crowd broke up, realizing that the crisis, the excitement was over. Only the car was still to be looked at, one door open, one shut, the top still shining in the sunlight.

"I wonder she didn't get out. Could 'ave," said one of the crowd.

"Yea, maybe she was knocked unconscious, or drunk, you never know."

Unconscious, or drunk, Marion Hughes, night superintendent of St. Jude's Hospital, would never be able to tell them, for the crowd, including the two boys and the policeman, had only to take one look at her when they opened that car door to know that she was very, very dead.

Sir James Hatfield, Dr. Galbraith, the senior physician, Gordon Mayes, the orthopaedic surgeon, the hospital secretary, and the chairman of the Management Committee, Sir Jeremy Hasler, were all seated in the board room, round the large table. They had just had coffee brought them and were waiting for the senior pathologist. He had asked them to meet him there, intimating that he had found something disturbing when doing the autopsy on Marion Hughes. So they waited.

"Strange business," said Gordon Mayes. "Funny woman. I never liked her particularly. I thought she was efficient and would have been an efficient driver. Must have skidded, I suppose."

"Skidded on what? There was no ice; it was a bit damp, and it was early morning—but I shouldn't have thought . . ." The rasping tone of Sir James's voice made Gordon Mayes look at him curiously. He watched him pick up his cup to sip his coffee and noticed with surprise that his hand was shaking visibly.

"Well, it could have been anything: loose gravel, leaves. It's easily done, especially if your tyres aren't all that hot." The hospital secretary, sensing a tension in the air, was trying to relieve it.

"If I know Marion Hughes, her tyres would be perfect," said Dr. Galbraith and went on, "Whatever else she was, not particularly likeable, not particularly beloved by the staff, she was efficient. I'd vouch for that whatever she coped with—car, hospital, theatre—it would be well done, if bitchily." He suddenly realized what he'd said and looked round self-consciously. After all, the woman was dead—he shouldn't have said that, but no one appeared to react.

At that moment the pathologist walked into the room.

"Coffee, Stan?" said Gordon Mayes. He seemed the least affected of anyone.

"Yes, yes thanks," said the pathologist and sat down at the table. He was holding a long sheet of paper in his hand. He put it down on the table for the moment and took the proffered cup of coffee, sipped it, and then looked round at the assembled men.

"This is rather a difficult and delicate situation," he said.

"The findings of the autopsy"—he looked again at the paper —"on Miss Hughes have been rather puzzling."

"Why puzzling?" asked the orthopaedic surgeon. "Why puzzling? She died of drowning. Or did something happen to her before? Did she have a brain haemorrhage or a black-out or something?"

"Neither." The pathologist glanced down at his notes again. "I found her to be a healthy woman, heart, lungs, cranium, everything normal—except the stomach contents."

"The stomach contents?" said Gordon Mayes. "The stomach contents, what?"

"What did he say, the stomach contents?" said the senior physician, Dr. Whitehouse, cupping his hand behind his ear. He was slightly deaf but would seldom admit it.

"Let him get on," said Sir James irritably, and the senior physician leaned back in his chair offended.

The pathologist went on. "The deceased had obviously just drunk a cup of coffee. There was no other food in the stomach, but there was a large quantity of Phenobarbitone, large enough to cause her . . . Well, large enough to make her driving less efficient than usual. She might well have been dizzy, particularly if she were not in the habit of taking Nembutal. There was also aspirin in the stomach contents in a very small quantity, not in proportions that would affect the deceased."

"I thought Nembutal, Seconal, the Phenobarbs were out now. I thought they confused old people and few were used. I know I don't give them on my ward. Are they . . . ?"

"Some are dispensed on the wards if the old people are used to them, but, as you say, they are not used in many cases now. Mogadon seems to be the fashionable sleeping pill at the moment. Of course there will have to be an investigation to see if any are missing from the pharmacy."

"How much had she taken?" asked Dr. Whitehouse, leaning forward, his hands clasped on the table in front of him.

"Well, the stomach content showed about fifteen grains, and she had ingested it shortly before. What I can't quite understand is that there was no sign of the material the capsules are made of. As you know, it takes a little time for them to dissolve. This, of course, would make the effect come on rather more quickly. She must, however, have got her car out of the parking lot quite easily and driven as far as the river road before . . . It makes me wonder: did she take the powder out of the capsules? Or was she able to get this substance in powder form? Or . . . ?" He looked round at the assembled consultants and administrator questioningly. "Or was the powder somehow given her . . . ?"

"Given her? What do you mean? Administered to her without her knowing? But that's murder," said Gordon Mayes.

"Oh, come, come," said the pathologist, "I was hardly suggesting that. She may herself have decided to take the powder rather than the capsules, knowing that it would act more quickly. That is, if she were an addict. There's a lot to find out. We've got to find out whether there is any Nembutal missing from the pharmacy, just how much is being given out to patients, whether indeed the lady was an addict. It's a nasty business. I've got a feeling that Marion Hughes might not have been aware that she was taking the Phenobarbitone. I can't see why she herself should take it just before she got into her car. I don't know the woman . . . It's rather jumping to conclusions to suspect foul play at this juncture . . . What do you think?"

"I've known her for some time on night duty. She's not the type . . . what do you think, Jimmy? Not the type to . . . not an addict, surely?" He looked across at Sir James.

"No, I wouldn't have thought so."

"Well, you knew her better than anyone really. She even scrubbed up for you, you told me. The night that that patient was . . . you remember, the one that . . . Lady Something or other," said Gordon Mayes.

"Well, yes, I knew her, but only on duty. She wasn't a personal friend," said Sir James, a pompous note creeping into his voice.

Dr. Galbraith looked at him curiously, remembering his remark in the theatre, remembering too that someone had told him that Jimmy had recently taken Miss Hughes out to dinner, but he said nothing.

"Well," said the pathologist getting up. "There's the report, gentlemen," and he laid it on the table. "I guess we go on from there. I can't say she died from natural causes, that's for sure. But why she took so much Phenobarbitone just before she was going to drive her car is, to put it mildly, a bit strange. We shall have to tell the police, I'm afraid. They know, of course, about her death; they had to dredge the car out. They know that much, but at the moment it's on the books as a pure accident. I'm afraid I can't let it stay that way."

"No, of course you can't. We'll have to put it in a formal report. What a scandal this is going to cause. I do hate this sort of thing," said Eric Hall, the hospital secretary. "Any scandal attached to a hospital sticks for ages and anything like this will be taken up by the media and . . ."

"Haven't come across it much so far, thank God," said Gordon Mayes.

The remark was innocent, but Sir James said testily, "I don't think any of us have, but you do read about things happening in hospitals . . . The public doesn't forget for a while."

"No, but there it is. I'm afraid it will have to be reported, investigated, the distribution of drugs in the hospital looked into, any shortages, etc.—you know the scene," said the pathologist. He walked towards the door. At that moment it opened and Nigel Denton put his head round.

"They're waiting for us in theatre, sir," he said to Gordon Mayes, and looked curiously round the assembled group.

"O.K. I'm coming now," said the surgeon. "There's nothing further you want me for then?" he asked.

"No, not at the moment. All that will come later," the hospital secretary answered.

Gordon Mayes followed Denton out of the door and they made their way towards the theatre.

"Everything all right, sir?" asked Nigel, looking curiously at his chief.

"For the moment," said Gordon Mayes. "Let's get on with the job in hand, eh?" Nigel Denton nodded but looked as if he would like to ask more, then thought better of it and they continued up to the operating-theatre.

The evening after the morning Marion Hughes had been found was dark and drizzling. Hiram Jones walked along the road to the hospital like an automaton. His thoughts were chaotic. He wished to God he hadn't got to go on duty. At home, when he had awakened after the last short catnap of a series which had made up most of the day, he had almost decided to ring in and say he would have to be off sick, got diarrhoea and vomiting or some such thing, and yet he had to know . . . So, here he was, on the way.

Spring seemed to have disappeared completely, and the wind blew the fine rain into his face. He was walking by a newsagent's close to the hospital gates, and he noticed a torn paper flapping in the wet breeze. On it had been hastily scrawled in thick felt Biro: HOSPITAL SISTER FOUND DROWNED TRAPPED IN CAR.

Hiram stopped, oblivious at the moment of the weather. Was it . . . ? he thought. But there were other hospitals in the country, other sisters. He read the notice again as it blew disconsolately, as the drizzling rain made the blue ink run a little more. When was that put there? This morning? They must have found . . . He hurried along the road to the hospital gate and almost ran along the courtyard to the door, opened it, and banged it behind him.

"That's it, keep the hospital nice and quiet for the patients' sake," said the switchboard operator through her open door as he went in.

"Was it, that placard I saw on the way, was it . . . ?" he asked the operator, his breathing fast, almost laboured. She nodded.

"Yea, old Hughesie. Found the car in the river. She must have driven off the road or skidded. B.I.D.," she said—hospital jargon for brought in dead.

"Where were you when she came in? Were you on duty?" Hiram was almost stuttering in his anxiety to learn the facts.

"Yeah, my day on, wasn't it?" She looked at her watch. "I'm nearly due off. Not nice, is it? I didn't like her, I mean, still . . ."

"Well, what happened? Did you hear? Did she skid or what?" The operator looked at him and then looked round to see if there was anybody else near. Then she lowered her voice in a conspiratorial whisper: "Well," she said, "there was a lot of to-ing and fro-ing and they did a pretty smart autopsy on her. I reckon there's more to it than just a motor accident. You know what I mean?"

"No, I don't know what you mean," said Hiram.

"Well, we shall see," the switchboard operator said airily.

"But I reckon I heard something on the phone about stomach content." She looked at Hiram slyly.

"Stomach content? You mean . . . ? What's that got to do with it? Tell me, what did they say? Really, I mean, or are you just playing about . . . just guessing? It said on the placard outside the newsagent's that she was drowned."

"Ye—ah, well, they found her car in the river, and of course she was dr-ow-ned, but I'm telling you what I heard, and I'm not supposed to, so I'm not saying any more."

She shut the books in front of her with a bang, got up, and at that moment the night operator walked in. Hiram left them to it, looked at his watch, saw that it was two minutes after the time he should be on duty, and ran up the stairs quicker than usual to Stenton ward. Before he started the report, he asked the day staff nurse what had happened.

"Haven't a clue," said the staff nurse. "Except that some kids found her and reported it to the police station. Well, they saw the car, she was in it all right; bit of an uproar I can tell you. All very secret. Of course you know how secret things are in hospitals. Anyway, there it is, no more Marion Hughes. Can't say I'm sorry for one. Mind you, I wouldn't have her drowned like that, you know, but still . . ."

"What made the car . . . ? I mean, why did they think . . . ? What made the car go down?"

"Ah-h." The staff nurse looked up at him, a quizzical expression on his face. "Drink, someone said. But at that time in the morning? I ask you. Well, they'd say anything about anyone, wouldn't they?"

Hiram was aching to know more, but the staff nurse wanted to get off, so it was difficult, and the report rattled on, and suddenly as the names were read out together with their condition, Hiram was brought back with a jerk to Mr. Butterworth. Had he found out his pills were missing?

"Mr. Brown, bed four, still incontinent, both faeces and

urine. Mr. Jones, still on eye drops, seems to be reacting well to them, blepharitis much better. Mr. Jason, I've put him in the corner, he's been a bit difficult today and maybe tonight he will be too, so if he needs anything get the house physician to order it. Personally I don't think he's written up for enough sedation and he may keep the whole ward awake. Mr. Butterworth . . ."

Hiram held his breath. Would he have reported the loss of his pills? He might have. He didn't want anybody to know that he'd got them, but he might have.

"Mr. Butterworth, comfortable day, not complaining. Mr. Amos, comfortable day, not complaining."

The report went on. Old Butterworth either hadn't noticed his pills were gone or had decided to say nothing about them. What could he say? He'd get in a row for having them, but on the other hand he could say he'd had something pinched and start a furore. But it looked as if he hadn't, thank God. He must have found out, though, that the bottle wasn't there. If he'd kept them all the time in that tissue box, he must have found out. Anyway, he hadn't said anything, or the report would have noted it.

One comfort, Marion Hughes wouldn't be able to report him. Then another horror passed through his mind: what if she'd taken them out of his pocket, when she went into the Casualty cloakroom? Supposing she'd seen them there, banged into his coat, felt in his pocket, taken the bottle out, and read the name on it? She'd know they were Butterworth's. Supposing she'd put them in her handbag and the handbag had kept the bottle dry and the label still . . . ? They could trace it back. God, what a mess. Had she already, before she'd . . . ? Had she told anybody what she'd found in his pocket? Oh, it was too much, just too much. But after all, he'd seen her in the canteen that morning, and she'd seen him, or he thought she had. Wouldn't she have mentioned it then? No, just like her, she'd hold it, ready to come out with it suddenly . . . She couldn't come out with it now. He felt very sick.

"Good night, then," the day staff nurse said. "Good night, and keep that old devil in the corner quiet for goodness' sake, or you're going to have hell."

Hiram nodded and stood in the middle of the ward as the day staff left, nodding good night as they went. He was determined to do his round quickly, not go into the kitchen and have his usual cup of tea that his junior probably was making now. No. He'd walk round straightaway to find out what old Butterworth would say to him.

"Good evening, Mr. Jones. Good evening, Mr. Cartwright." He stayed for a very short time at each bed, much shorter than usual, and arrived at Mr. Butterworth's bed almost breathless from the difficulty of keeping his emotions in check and listening to the ramblings of the old men at whose beds he had stopped.

"Evening, Mr. Butterworth," he said. "How are you then?"

Old Butterworth looked up from reading a paperback and pulled his glasses down his nose to see Hiram better. His little, blue watery eyes looked up at Hiram suspiciously.

"I'm all right, why shouldn't I be? I'm all right. I haven't wet the bed. I haven't done anything wrong. You don't usually come round as early as this. You usually chatter in the kitchen before you come and speak to the likes of us. What's the matter with you then?"

"Nothing, nothing," said Hiram hastily. "I just thought I'd get the round done earlier."

"What's happened to old bitchy Hughes, then?" said Butterworth. "Gone and drowned herself, I hear, drowned herself in the river, nice goings on. Don't wonder either; probably someone pushed her," he went on nastily.

"How did you know that anything had happened to her at all?" asked Hiram.

Old Butterworth put his hand up to his face and tapped the side of his nose with his finger.

"Not much I don't know, not much I don't know. Am I getting any Nembutal tonight, or do I have to take my own?" he asked, his eyes still fixed on Hiram.

"I'll give you some," said Hiram hastily. It couldn't be that he hadn't found out that the bottle was missing, it couldn't be; of all the luck. The old man was always taking out tissues and cleaning his glasses or blowing his nose. Hiram looked involuntarily towards the tissue box, and old Butterworth followed his gaze. He picked up the box and put it under the sheet in front of him.

"Oh-h, so you know where they are, do you? Well you just keep your great mitts off them, that's all. I didn't want you to know where they were. They disappeared and I found them under the bed, must have dropped them under there. But you're not supposed to know I've got them at all, are you?" he said.

"That's a stupid place to put them," said Hiram, "if that's where they are. No, I don't care where you keep them. I don't want them, as long as you don't take an overdose. And how did they get under the bed?"

"Suppose I dropped them. Anyway I got out of bed and trod on the bottle luckily," said old Butterworth craftily. "But I'm not taking these, not while you've got some to give me."

"Are you sure they're still there?" It slipped out before Hiram had a chance to think how to ask the old man about the bottle more obliquely. He cursed himself; what a senseless remark. The old man hastily withdrew the box from underneath the sheet and pushed his hand in the end.

"Yes," he said, "they're still here all right." And he drew

out the plastic bottle with the capsules in it and shook them in front of Hiram's nose.

"And I'll put them somewhere else, under me piller, in case somebody finds them. You knew they were in there," he said. "Cheeky devil."

"How did—I mean, have they been there all the time?" asked Hiram.

"Of course they 'ave, 'cept when I dropped them under the bed, like I was telling you." He looked thoughtful. "I don't remember doing that, though. If they cleaned the place properly, they'd 'ave found them. I trod on 'em when I got out of bed, to pass water, see, so I picked 'em up pretty quickish I can tell you and put 'em back in me tissues. Dunno whether I shall keep 'em there, though." He glanced at Hiram and away.

"How many are there in the bottle?" Hiram asked.

The old man held the bottle up to the light. "Not all that many; take more than that to kill me off. Reckon my daughter's taken some out, 'case I poisoned meself. Not that she'd mind," he said.

Hiram too looked at the bottle. Certainly there looked to be far fewer than when he had counted them on the kitchen table. It looked as if about twelve or fifteen were gone. He tried to remember how the level of capsules had looked in the bottle after he'd put the twenty in the envelope, but he couldn't.

"Let me count them," he said.

"No." Butterworth clenched the bottle firmly in his fist and thrust it under the clothes. "I'm not going to let you touch 'em. What do you want to count 'em for anyway?"

"Well, I'd feel happier, that's all. I don't want you to forget and take two more when you've already taken them. You can, you know, with these kind of pills."

"I shan't take 'em at all if you give me the hospital ones,

like you should," said Mr. Butterworth and looked at him again slyly. He liked Hiram. "All right, I'll count 'em if you want me to. I'll do it."

He unscrewed the cap of the bottle, tipped the Nembutal into his hand. The little capsules made their usual dry rattle as they fell into the old palm. He propped the bottle up beside his hand and began to count.

Hiram calculated rapidly. Wherever the bottle had been didn't matter, but had anybody taken any of the capsules out? He'd know now. The old man counted slowly, and Hiram shuffled his feet with impatience. There had been fifty-six as far as he could remember, and he'd taken out twenty and put them in the envelope—that made thirty-six. There should be thirty-six; the old man stopped counting at twenty-five.

"Twenty-five. Thought there was more than that, but it's a nice little few." It was obvious that old Butterworth had never known originally how many there were in the bottle.

How the hell had the bottle got back to Butterworth? Hiram watched the old man screw the top on firmly, thrust the bottle into the tissue box, and then push the box down under the sheet and hold it firmly on his stomach.

"If this bottle disappears I shall know where it went," he said.

"Why should it disappear?" said Hiram.

"You never know. Things do disappear in a hospital, and sometimes you get 'em back, but not always," said Mr. Butterworth.

Did the old man know the bottle had been missing? Was the story of finding it under the bed true? Hiram couldn't tell. His mind again was in this awful turmoil, going round and round like a treadmill. Where had the missing capsules gone? At any rate he was in the clear; they were back and he was supposed to know nothing about it. He changed the subject.

"Did your daughter come today?" he asked, just for something to say.

"No, she didn't, that bloody girl. I mean she never turned up. She said she was coming with her husband and the kids; not one of them came, it's not good enough. The longer you're in here, the more they forget you. Still a nice Social Services lady came and had a chat with me; she had a cold. She was nice, though, quite nice."

"Social Services lady?" said Hiram. He presumed Butterworth meant the social medical worker.

"Yes, well that's what she said she was, Social Services. She didn't ask me much, though, not about me pension or anything."

Hiram nodded vaguely and went on to the next bed. He just couldn't sort it all out. He'd better get the round done and think about it afterwards.

As he walked down the middle of the ward to the kitchen, he thought: Social Services lady, who the hell was that? Could be, well, he wouldn't be able to find out until the day staff came on in the morning. Perhaps not then, but he'd ask.

Jane Creasey came into Casualty at ten o'clock. She had been away the whole day and was feeling slightly pleased with herself. She had been short-listed for the Casualty post for which she had applied and felt fairly sure of having got it on her second visit to the hospital. The people who had interviewed her had been pleasant, and it was obvious that they thought her qualifications were what was required for that particular post.

She was glad, too, that she had managed to make it back in time to get on duty in Casualty without having to ask a further favour of Nigel Denton, although she felt sure he would have done another night for her if she had asked him.

The night casualty staff nurse had summoned her to Casualty to look at a badly cut finger. The cut was long and deep. The patient was a woman. She had done it opening a can, the usual household injury.

She lay on the table, a board thrust under her to support her arm. The junior nurse wheeled the trolley up to Dr. Creasey and she sutured the finger quickly and expertly. The woman lay there looking slightly pale, her face turned away from the doctor, but apparently feeling hardly anything, as the local anaesthetic dulled the needle thrust to and fro.

The casualty nurse stood gazing into space. It was a small injury; she hoped they wouldn't get many more that night. She wanted to write some letters, and a slight quarrel with her boy-friend had made her determined to write a little love note to him. She didn't want to lose him. He was a nice boy, and she wasn't all that flush with boy-friends.

"Any news of Miss Hughes?" asked Dr. Creasey, as she walked out of the theatre, leaving the nurse to bandage the finger and give the woman her injection of penicillin and anti-tetanus.

The staff nurse turned from the desk at which she was writing and said, "Oh, yes." She looked at the theatre door and then went on in a low voice. "Haven't you heard? They found her car in the river. She was in it, must have been there all day and all night. Some kids saw it, reported it to the police, and they went and fished her out. They did an autopsy on her, bit of a hurry. Don't know why; she must have drowned. There's all sorts of rumours."

"Rumours? What do you mean?" asked Dr. Creasey.

"Well, there was nothing to skid on, but she went off the road apparently, down that grass slope, you know, opposite

Wilton's factory, and into the river. They said there was nothing to make her skid; tyres were all right."

"Well, why . . . ?" Dr. Creasey looked curiously at the girl and thought how little she was moved and hoped the lack of sorrow was something that wouldn't happen if ever she met with a fatal accident.

"Well, I mean, she could have been drunk, couldn't she? Or doped or something. They say she had a headache. She could have had a brain haemorrhage, like Mrs. Upton said, and gone off the road. Apparently she took some aspirins before she went. I went down to the canteen this evening. Mrs. Upton was right proud of herself. The police have asked her questions already. Well, she was the last person to see her alive, I suppose, that's what she said, but I said, well, how do you know that?"

"Good God. Poor woman. Drowned in her car in the river. That must have been a horrible end," said Dr. Creasey.

"Yes," the nurse said. "Must have been, but there you are; couldn't have happened to a nastier person," and she smiled up at Miss Creasey, and the doctor found herself shocked.

She left Casualty and went along to the Common Room, where George Hayward was sitting in his usual slumped position watching the television.

"George, what's this about Marion Hughes?" she asked.

"Hallo, love," said George, looking up at her. "Get your job then?"

"Yes, I think so. But what's this about Marion Hughes?"

"Oh, it's filtered down from the great ones to us lesser ones. Apparently she slewed off the road," said George.

"I know that, but why did she slew off the road?" said Dr. Creasey, hastily interrupting him.

"They thought all sorts of things at first," said George. "That business of the busy night in Casualty and Mrs. Upton saying she took some aspirins or something before she went.

Well, it wasn't only aspirins they found inside her stomach but a hell of a lot of Phenobarbitone. She must have doped herself up before she went out, silly fool."

"Phenobarbitone?" said Dr. Creasey incredulously. "Where did she get it? From the pharmacy?"

"Nope, none missing apparently, expect she had a stock. There's a lot we don't know about that woman, but why the hell she should take a load on like that before driving her car, I can't think. Apparently nobody saw her leave her parking place, but she didn't bump any cars or anything, so she couldn't have been that stoned. She got as far as the river, and bingo—she was gone. What did she want to do that for? Phenobarbitone, that much before you're going to drive a car. Strange . . ." He looked up suddenly. "Foul play is suspected, my dear," he said.

"Oh, come on, foul play, how could . . . ?" Dr. Creasey said, looking at him with round eyes.

"That dame had got a lot of things on lots of people. There was Sir James for one; there was something going on there. What, I don't know. Nigel, he wasn't keen on her."

At that moment Nigel walked into the Common Room. "Wasn't keen on whom? I can guess . . ." He sank down beside the other two, looking tired and ill.

George Hayward got up and turned the volume of the television down. The figures on the screen went on speaking, opening and shutting their mouths like goldfish in a bowl.

"I hear you've got that job, congratulations." Nigel looked across at Dr. Creasey and she blushed with pleasure.

"Yes, I think it's almost certain. It's a more senior post than this. Not a consultancy you know, Nigel, but it might lead to one. I'm rather pleased."

"I'm jolly sure you must be," said Nigel, then turned back to George. "Do you want that thing on? I mean without the sound, it's irritating," he said.

"How much did she take, Marion Hughes I mean?" Dr. Creasey asked.

"As far as I can get out of old Mayes, twelve or fifteen grains." Nigel sounded as if he didn't want to speak about it.

"How many capsules is that? Don't use the stuff now, not much anyway."

Nigel Denton didn't answer but continued staring at the figures on the television screen.

"Um-m, ten or so, can't remember." George Hayward pursed his lips. "I never use the stuff either. It might come back, though. You know how they are. Drugs come into fashion and then someone says it confuses old people, that you get withdrawal symptoms, and they're gone. Then they're back again. I can remember drugs," he said reminiscently, "in my short life as a doctor, that came in with a bang and went out with a whimper. Still don't really see Phenobarb coming back."

"Well, it's Schedule One. They'll know if some's missing, for goodness' sake," said Nigel, his irritability obvious.

"Oh, they've checked that already, checked with the wards, checked with the drug book, checked with the pharmacy. None missing, not a capsule. Very well kept books, too, I'm glad to say. It would have been a great disgrace if we'd have been slipshod about it. No, that's O.K.," George said.

"Strange, isn't it, nobody's said they're sorry, not to me anyway, nobody," said Dr. Creasey.

"Well, for God's sake, love," said George Hayward, "look what she did to everybody. I mean, there's you, reporting that angina and treating you like a . . . Well, we won't go into that. We can forget it all. She never had much to say to me, for some reason. I seemed to keep out of her bad books, but I'm sure if I'd put a step wrong . . . I doubt there's a nurse in this hospital tonight, or doctor come to that, who gives a damn. It's only the scandal that worries them. Sir James won't like it of course. He likes to keep the scandal sheets clean, especially now that he's after the Hon. Madeleine."

"I didn't know about her. Someone he's . . ." said Dr. Creasey.

"After the proper time, after the proper time, dear, a year you know, she'll be Lady Hatfield," said George.

"Oh, I didn't know about that. I thought Marion Hughes had her eye on him," said Nigel.

"She may have had, but he hadn't got his eyes on her, I'll bet," said George. "Not enough money for one thing. He likes the loot, does our Sir James."

"Well, I'm going to rest," said Dr. Creasey. She obviously didn't like this gossip.

"Do that, get as much sleep as you can, and congrats. on the new job, I really mean it," said George, and Nigel repeated his congratulations.

The casualty officer turned round to him. "Thanks, and I'm sorry about Marion Hughes. No matter what, I feel sorry about it now," she said and walked out of the room.

"Nice dame," said George to Nigel, and Nigel nodded abstractedly.

"Not the marrying kind, though," George went on, "do you think? I hope she gets a consultancy. This Casualty job, it's quite good, you know, and the status that goes with it will be good for a dame like our Dr. Creasey. It'll give her more confidence."

"I don't think she liked us talking like that about the dear departed," said Nigel lightly.

"No, but then she's nicer-natured than we are," said George. "Shall I go over and get a pack from the pub?"

"Do that," said Nigel, and, as George left the room, he thought of what Dr. Creasey had said: no one was sorry. Well he certainly wasn't. He went over and switched the volume up on the television, then returned and sat down, but it was obvious that he was not taking any notice of what was being acted out on the small screen in front of him.

The staff nurse on night duty in the women's surgical ward looked up in surprise as Staff Carmichael tapped the ward door, asking for permission to come in. She nodded briskly and Carmichael came up to her desk.

"I just wanted to ask you something," Carmichael said diffidently, her long nose, slightly red at the end, twitching a little as it always did, particularly as now when she was nervous.

The staff nurse of the women's surgical ward nodded absently. "O.K., but don't let's talk in here. We'll wake them up. Let's go into the kitchen," she said. They walked together quietly down the darkened ward, past the sleeping women, past the one in the corner, with a drip suspended on a stand beside her and a tube leading down into her arm, her eyes wide open, looking into space. This made the staff nurse pause and go to her side and whisper something to her. She nodded, and the surgical staff nurse joined Carmichael again and they went into the kitchen.

"She's all right, had her gall bladder out today. Nice woman, doesn't make a fuss. She might not get much sleep tonight, though. You look pretty rough," she said as Carmichael took a crumpled tissue from her pocket and took off her glasses, revealing more fully her red-rimmed eyes. She rubbed at the glasses industriously and then put them back on.

"Yes, I'm not feeling all that good. I'm sorry to interrupt you; it's my rest hour. I thought I'd just come and ask you something." Carmichael looked with those anxious, flickering eyes at the surgical ward staff nurse, then sat down heavily on

a kitchen chair. "Hope you don't mind, Nurse James," she
burst out again.

"Oh, for goodness' sake, of course I don't mind. What's
the matter? What do you want?"

"It's about . . . well, partly about Miss Hughes, and
partly about the day post on this ward, Sister's post, you know
. . ."

"Oh, you mean Sister Grainger's leaving. I know. What
about it?"

"Well, I was wondering whether you'd heard anything
about anyone else being appointed, or applying—whether I'd
stand a chance if I applied? Are you going to try?"

"No, not me," said the night staff. "It suits me, this job on
night duty. I'm married, you see, and I get the four nights off.
They're worth having and in the long run it pays better. No, I
haven't applied. I know one or two who are thinking of applying, and, of course, there will be some from other hospitals."

"I was thinking I'd like to apply now . . ." Staff Carmichael's voice sounded unusually firm.

"Now?" The staff nurse looked at her questioningly.

"Well, I wasn't expecting a very good report from Marion
Hughes, and now she's gone, well . . ."

"Who was? After all, she'd have given Florence Nightin-
gale a downer. There can't be many people in the hospital
who are sorry. A nasty way to go, though. Personally, I never
had much truck with her. It was usually old Norman did her
rounds here," said Nurse James.

Carmichael looked suddenly confused, as if she hadn't been
listening, then nodded vaguely.

"Yes, I think I'll try, I'll apply. After all, why not? The day
sister thought I was all right. It was just Miss Hughes." Her
voice ended almost on a hysterical note.

"All right then, apply; but steady down, old girl. If you
don't get it, there are other sister's posts coming up, don't you

worry; and as you say, now the thorn in the flesh is removed you might stand as good a chance as any other." She didn't really believe it, as she looked at Carmichael's white face, and dark-circled, red-rimmed eyes, and the hand that trembled, as she put it up to push her glasses back on her nose.

She's in a state, Nurse James thought. Shouldn't be ward sister. She should be in a psychiatric ward, I should have thought, and not as a nurse. And why doesn't she get those damn glasses fixed? Just then a buzzer went and she said, "Sorry, love, I have to go now, but as I said, have a try. Cheerio then." She walked out of the kitchen and into the ward, and Carmichael could hear her murmuring something to the patient who had buzzed.

I will, thought Carmichael, I will put my application in. She can't have left any notes about me, just can't have. She didn't expect to die. I must talk to Norman. I must talk to anybody who will do me any good. Now she's dead, she's dead, and she can do nothing to me, nothing, I'm certain.

Carmichael felt again this tide rising in her, as it had the night she had fingered the knife and several times since. She remembered the knife again as she walked out of the brightly lighted kitchen into the more dimly lighted corridor and up to the rest-room. She sat down in a chair and put her feet up automatically on another and tried to relax. She couldn't. Thoughts came crowding in on her. One moment she felt elated, the next depressed and frightened. She had heard from so many people when she arrived on night duty this evening of how Marion Hughes's car had been fished up.

She sat there, picturing it dangling in the air, with the filthy water of that river pouring out of the sides, and then landing gently, or perhaps not so gently, on the road.

Police dashing about, throwing open the door. She wished she'd been there. Not the neat Miss Hughes with a bun coiled on the nape of her white neck, lipstick on perfectly, and the tiny suggestion of eye-shadow, in her neat suit, with those patent court shoes making her feet look slender, and her ankles, too.

Carmichael smiled. No, none of that. She would have been covered with that filthy slime. She wished she'd been able to see her in the mortuary when she came in. They'd have had to wash her all off, take off that suit, everything. She'd just be there, naked. Miss Hughes naked, with her hair soaked with mud, that's how she would have liked to have seen her. She hadn't had the chance, but she could visualize it now. She lay back and almost relaxed in delight at the thought . . . Then, they'd have to cut her up; she'd seen post-mortems.

Suddenly her mood of relaxation changed. She felt quite confident, quite certain that she'd get the post of sister on the women's surgical. She only had to apply, that's all. Forget it, they couldn't refuse her. She had all the experience necessary. She looked at her watch; a quarter of an hour left of her rest hour. She sat forward and felt excited and sure of herself. Why did I go and ask that night staff nurse, she thought; it was foolish, there was no need for it. Then her head started to ache again and her thoughts changed. Did I go and ask her? Or did I . . . ? No, she couldn't remember, it was stupid. Had she been to the surgical ward, or was she just going? She shrugged her shoulders. There was no need anyway to worry about it. She would get the post; there was no need to ask anyone. It was an odd feeling, though, this certainty. A tension headache came back. It didn't seem to react to any of the pills she was taking; she'd go down to the canteen and have a cup of coffee. If she was a bit late back on the ward, well it didn't matter now. Her junior must just put up with it.

She felt completely invincible. She walked across the restroom, her head held unusually high, nodding to one or two sleepy nurses reclining in chairs. She walked out of the door and made her way down the stairs to the canteen, and on her way she said loudly to herself, "I can do anything and I'll prove it."

The stomach content findings were reported to the police, and the usual further forensic investigations began. It seemed to the staff that they went on, and on, and on.

For three days there were policemen and inspectors appearing suddenly and asking questions of the receptionist, the switchboard operator, and others. Sometimes the C.N.O. accompanied them, looking ruefully at the person who was to be questioned and giving a little shrug of the shoulders, as if to say, it can't be helped. But nobody minded. It was exciting.

The detective inspector was closeted a long time with the senior nursing officer. Everybody knew that, but nobody knew what passed between them. Miss Norman, too, was questioned, but she was more outgoing and told people what they'd asked her.

"Oh, he just said, did I know if old Hughes took drugs, suffered from nervous tension, anything like that, and of course I didn't. I didn't know she took drugs, but she must have, I reckon, though why she took them then . . ."

It was irksome, but in the end it seemed to mean nothing. Again all the Schedule One drugs were checked, and none found to be missing. It was a good thing, for the hospital's good name depended on that kind of thing, and had a lot of any of the drugs been missing there would have been more questions, more trouble at Management Committee level, and God knows what. But no, nothing was found to be wrong. If Marion Hughes had got Nembutal in her stomach, it must, they decided, have been her own. Her general practitioner was asked, but he had never prescribed any; not that that meant a lot. As he said, if you were a determined addict you could buy Nembutal without a great deal of trouble.

But as Norman said, one couldn't imagine Marion Hughes doing that kind of thing, buying Nembutal, yet one knew so little about her, how could one say? No, it was a mystery.

The result of the inquest seeped through to the hospital pretty quickly and then appeared in the local paper a few days later: DEATH BY MISADVENTURE. The affair was already beginning to retreat into the distance.

Norman was made acting senior night superintendent. Everybody was pleased about that, and an appointment would, of course, follow later for her post. Gradually the whole thing receded more and more into the background, and five or six days later it was just a talking point, and little more, and that more so on night duty than on day, for Marion Hughes had been a stranger to day duty, except for her early morning grumbles, about how she had found wards the night before. They had listened to the night staff's moans about her, but they didn't really know her, only as a bit of a nuisance at report time.

When one of the gardeners cut through the cable of his hedge trimmer and was brought in nearly dead with a couple of porters holding him down, that took over on day duty as a nine days' wonder. He recovered but he had pushed Marion Hughes farther into the background.

Nights later, Atkins came into the canteen at his rest hour and found several of his mates there.

"Hi, folks," he said and poked his head round the canteen kitchen door. "Coffee and buns, love," he said to Mrs. Upton.

"You'll get buns," she called back, and he laughed and came over to the table and sat down.

"I'm sick of not having something with me coffee. I think I'll start bringing something in," he said. He looked across at his other junior from the geriatric ward opposite Stenton.

"What are you eating, anyway?"

"Buns, stupid. I bring them in."

"Give us one then," said Atkins.

"Nothing doing," said the other nurse and proceeded to munch into his second bun.

"Friendship, that's what I like on night duty," said Atkins. "Friendship, nothing like it."

"Well, why don't you go on day duty then?" said the bun eater morosely.

"What, now old Hughes is dead, after I've so cleverly polished her off? You must be joking."

"You never, you haven't got the gumph to do a thing like that. It was me," said the bun eater. "I got these capsules, see, and I dropped them into her tea as Mrs. Upton was taking it upstairs to her office. Isn't that right, Mrs. Upton?" he asked as Mrs. Upton emerged from the kitchen with a cup of coffee for Atkins.

"No it isn't. She didn't get any tea the night she died. I told the police that. It was that Casualty thing, remember? Anyway, you shouldn't joke about things like that, it's not nice," said Mrs. Upton, and she turned and walked out of the canteen and back into the kitchen, her fat bottom waggling with disapproval.

"Case disproved," said a pretty young nurse from the orthopaedic ward. She went on, "I did it, actually, I did it. Let me see now. Yes, you see she felt the heat in Casualty. She had this faintness come over her at the sight of blood. Well, let's face it, she hadn't seen a patient in years, had she? So I said, 'Wait a minute, Miss Hughes, I'll fix you up.' I got some brandy and I put some Nembutal in it, and I said, 'Drink it down, dear.' And she did, just like a lamb, and that was the end of her."

"Ah yes, some hopes," cried several of the nurses, getting more interested in the topic now, and another one spoke up,

"That wouldn't have been any good. When she got to the bottom of the brandy it would feel like pebbles with those capsules; she'd have spat them out. As a murderer you're use-less. Actually I did it."

"How?" They were all joining in the game now and en-joying it.

"We-e-ll . . ." This nurse obviously hadn't got any ideas in her head for she paused too long.

Someone else chimed in, a male nurse, this time from men's surgical. "No, it was me," he said. "She did this round, see, and just as we got to the door she came over all queer, and she said, 'Can I have a drink of water, nurse?' and I said, 'Oh, certainly.' And she said, 'I've been working so hard in Casu-alty, I'm quite worn out and I haven't had my tea.' So I said, 'I know, I'll make you a sandwich, Miss Hughes,' and she said, 'That would be lovely.' "

There were cries of "I bet, I can just see it," and someone added, "Old Hughesie eating on the ward, some hopes." One of them looked suggestively across at Carmichael, who was sitting silent, but she dropped her eyes and would not meet the challenge.

"Shut up," the speaker went on. "In she came, into the kitchen, and I cut her two thin slices of bread and butter, took the crusts off of course, then I went out to the medicine trolley and got this Nembutal, and I made her a Nembutal sandwich, and she ate it, and drank her water, and never said a word. She never even asked me what the flavouring was I put in, and off she went. You see, you've got me to thank," he said, and there was a general roar of laughter.

"Well, I've heard of a chip butty but never a Nembutal butty," said someone, and there was more laughter.

"You're all wrong. It was old Uppie in there in the kitchen," said another nurse. "Tell you what, she'd broken her cup, and that was the end . . . She decided she'd got to be done . . ."

"If I'd broken her tea cup I'd have taken the Nembutal myself, if I'd had any," said another voice. This time the laughter was cut across by Carmichael.

"You're all wrong," she said. "I did it. I did it myself. It was simple. She was down here, in the canteen, and I had this Nembutal you see."

There were cries of, "Oh, yes, in your pocket, in your handbag, always carry a bottle, fancy!"

"I had this Nembutal," Carmichael went on, and her voice was calm and expressionless. "And I emptied the capsules out into this cup of coffee in front of me, and when Miss Hughes was called out for a minute, I changed cups. Simple. She drank it down and then went out. Oh yes, I did it."

"That's the best we've heard yet, Agatha Christie," said Atkins. "The best we've had yet. You always carry a murder weapon around with you, do you, like a bottle of Nembutal, or a carving knife? I bet."

"No I don't," said Carmichael. The mention of the carving knife made her shake again. "I just happened to have one—bottle I mean—that night."

"Oh yeah," said Atkins, "just happened to have one. Anybody else got a bottle in their pocket? Just so I know before I drink this coffee," he said, and there was more laughter and barracking and Carmichael was forgotten.

"Well, I tell you this; her death didn't cause much grief, did it? Here we are all joking about doing it. Disgusting as old Uppie says, isn't it?"

"No, it isn't disgusting. She was a right bitch and we all

know it. She caused more trouble in five minutes in this hospital than anyone else in a lifetime."

"Yes, I've got to admit that, and if I found out that she didn't take the Nembutal herself, and somebody else gave it to her and made her car slew off the road and killed her, well I'd give 'em a medal."

"Perhaps they wouldn't want a medal. Perhaps they only wanted a bit of peace, maybe promotion." Carmichael's precise voice cut across the laughter again, but the voice, even though it was so clear and precise, was drowned by the laughter.

Morning came, and the end of that night, and the sun shone again on the façade of St. Jude's, and spring seemed to have come back again, after the drizzling rain of the last few days.

Staff Nurse Carmichael walked down the front steps of the hospital to make her way to her bus and then on to her bed-sitting room. Somehow she felt, and indeed she looked, quite a different Nurse Carmichael. She walked with her head up and with a spring in her step, and she felt full of well-being.

As she walked towards the gate of the courtyard in front of the hospital, it went through her mind that it would be better not to go near Stenton ward, to keep well away from it. Old Mr. Butterworth might remember the "social worker." She thought again of his bewildered face as she'd approached, and drawn up a chair, and deposited the bottle under his bed—someone would find it. No, she wouldn't go near Stenton again, anyway she had no cause to.

She wasn't so keen on the women's surgical ward now; she didn't want to be sister there. She felt a change of hospital, a change of scene, might be better. Perhaps she'd apply for a

Casualty department, or an Out Patients' department—that would be even better, something where more people would see her, and she'd see more people. Yes, she didn't want to be hidden away in the night any more. She turned at the gate and looked back at the hospital, back at the pleasant façade and the green bust of Queen Victoria, who seemed to be beaming benignly down at her.

"They were amused when I told them," she said aloud, directing the remark to Queen Victoria, and then she finished, "But we were not amused, were we, we knew, didn't we?" And she turned on her heel and walked out of the big gate towards her bus.

87711

ABOUT THE AUTHOR

ANTHEA COHEN trained as a nurse at Leicester Royal Infirmary. For the past twenty-five years she has worked, on and off, in hospitals and as a private nurse. She has written on medicine and hospital life, been a columnist for *Nursing Mirror*, and has contributed regularly to *World Medicine*. She has published innumerable short stories and is a popular author of books for the teen-age market in the United States. *Angel Without Mercy* is her first crime novel.